THE GUARDIANS

E. ASTER
BUNNYMUND

AND THE WARRIOR EGGS

AT THE EARTH'S CORE!

E. Aster Bunnymund, last of the Pookas

THE GUARDIANS

E. ASTER
BUNNYMUND

AND THE WARRIOR EGGS
AT THE EARTH'S CORE!

WILLIAM JOYCE

A Caitlyn Dlouhy Book

ATHENEUM BOOKS FOR YOUNG READERS
NEW YORK • LONDON • TORONTO • SYDNEY • NEW DELHI

Atheneum Books for Young Readers

An imprint of Simon & Schuster Children's Publishing Division

1230 Avenue of the Americas, New York, New York 10020

This book is a work of fiction. Any references to historical events, real people, or real places are used fictitiously. Other names, characters, places, and events are products of the author's imagination, and any resemblance to actual events or places or persons, living or dead, is entirely coincidental.

For information about special discounts for bulk purchases, please contact Simon & Schuster Special Sales at 1-866-506-1949 or business@simonandschuster.com.

The Simon & Schuster Speakers Bureau can bring authors to your live event. For more information or to book an event, contact the Simon & Schuster Speakers Bureau at 1-866-248-3049 or visit our website at www.simonspeakers.com.

Also available in an Atheneum Books for Young Readers hardcover edition

Book design by Lauren Rille

The text for this book was set in Adobe Jenson Pro.

The illustrations for this book were rendered in a combination of charcoal, graphite, and digital media.

Manufactured in the United States of America

0718 MTN

First Atheneum Books for Young Readers paperback edition September 2018

10 9 8 7 6 5 4 3 2 1

The Library of Congress has cataloged the hardcover edition as follows:

Joyce, William, 1957–

E. Aster Bunnymund and the warrior eggs at the earth's core! / William Joyce.

p. cm. — (The Guardians ; 2)

Summary: E. Aster Bunnymund uses his martial arts skills, his network of tunnels, and the help of MiM, Sand Mansnoozy, and Nicholas St. North to battle the Nightmare King, Pitch, who has sent a venomous serpent to attack Bunnymund's royal guard of warrior eggs.

ISBN 978-1-4424-3050-1 (hc)

ISBN 978-1-4424-3051-8 (pbk)

ISBN 978-1-4424-4991-6 (eBook)

[1. Good and evil—Fiction. 2. Adventure and adventurers—Fiction. 3. Nightmares—Fiction. 4. Wizards—Fiction. 5. Heroes—Fiction. 6. Easter bunny—Fiction. 7. Eggs—Fiction.]

I. Title.

PZ7.J857Ead 2012 [Fic]—dc23   2011052122

———◄●►———

To my lovely wife,
Elizabeth,
the grandest lady in all the cosmos

———◄●►———

Contents

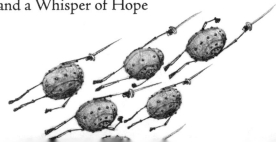

A Recap, a Prelude, and a Premonition of Terror

SINCE THE BATTLE OF the Nightmare King had been won, the planet seemed to be relatively quiet.

Katherine, North, and Ombric had stayed in the Himalayas with the Lunar Lamas. They knew Pitch and his Nightmare Armies would strike again. Pitch had escaped wearing the robot djinni's suit of armor and had vowed revenge against them all.

But the Man in the Moon had given North the magic sword that had belonged to his father. He had told them of four other relics from the Golden Age that could be helpful, perhaps essential, in defeating the Nightmare King, once and for all. But where Pitch was hiding or what they should do next was a puzzlement.

Similar questions were being pondered on a faraway island, in a secluded section of the Pacific Ocean. On this island there resided the most ancient, mysterious, and peculiar creature the world had ever known. Or not known, actually. Though he possessed extraordinary wisdom and power, he had given up on the comings and goings of history and humans. He had not allowed himself to be seen in living memory. This being, however, knew something was in the air. He knew about the battle of the Nightmare King, and he knew of Ombric and Pitch. He'd had dealings with them in the distant past. He could see and sense signs most unwelcome. Deep beneath the Earth (which was his realm), he heard ominous sounds. He kept to himself and liked it that way, but his animal instincts told him that, like it or not, he would once again be asked to help save the world he had so carefully cut himself off from.

His nose twitched. His massive ears flinched.

He wondered about the terrible battles to come and what, if any, part he would decide to play.

Our Heroes

North

Petrov

Nightlight

Ombric

Bear

Katherine

We Begin Our Story with a Story

IN THE HINTERLANDS OF eastern Siberia was the village where Katherine, North, and Ombric called home. The village of Santoff Claussen felt somewhat lonely without them, but a dozen or so adventurous children played in the enchanted forest that protected their homes from the outside world. The surrounding oak trees were among the largest in the world. Their massive trunks and limbs were a paradise for climbing.

Petter, a strong boy of twelve who imagined himself a daring hero, catapulted onto the porch of his favorite tree house. He landed just ahead of his little sister, Sascha. She was testing her latest invention: gloves and shoes that allowed her to scamper up a tree, like a squirrel. But Petter's catapult was faster.

"I'll beat you next time," Sascha said, hoping that a small engine on the heel of each shoe would do the trick.

She peered down at the clearing hundreds of feet below. The village's bear, a massive creature, loped around the perimeter of the clearing along with Petrov, the horse of Nicholas St. North. Sascha was wondering if she'd ever be allowed to ride Petrov when she spied Tall William, the first son of Old William, squatting on his heels, talking to a group of centipedes. The children of Santoff Claussen had begun to learn the easier insect languages (ant, worm, snail), but Tall William was the first to tackle the more difficult speech of centipede.

Sascha pressed a trumpet-shaped sound amplifier to her ear.

Tall William reported what the centipedes said, that all was well—Pitch, the Nightmare King, was nowhere to be seen. It was a warm summer day, but the memory of that terrible time when Pitch appeared in Santoff Claussen made Sascha shiver as if it were the darkest night in deepest winter.

Pitch had once been a hero of the Golden Age, an ancient time when Constellations ruled the universe. His name in those days long ago was General Kozmotis Pitchiner, and he had led the Golden Age Armies in capturing the Fearlings and Dream Pirates who plagued that era. These villains were wily creatures of darkness. When they escaped, they devoured the general's soul, and from that moment on, he hungered for the dreams of innocent children and was known simply as "Pitch." He was determined to drain the good from dreams until they became nightmares—every last one of them—so that the children of Earth and then other worlds would live in terror. And the dreams of the children of Santoff Claussen—who had never before known fear or wickedness—were the prizes he coveted most.

Sascha, like the other children of Santoff Claussen, had survived that terrifying night when Pitch's Fearlings had nearly captured them in the enchanted forest, thanks to a glimmering boy with a moonlit staff who drove back the inky marauders.

Now she climbed out onto a branch and hung by her knees, still holding the ear trumpet. *The world looks different upside down, but it sounds the same,* she thought.

Sascha listened once more, then lowered the

sound amplifier. The insects had said all was well. *Even so, what if Pitch and his Fearlings come back again?* She frowned, but before that thought could darken her mood, Petter called out for a new contest. "Race you to the clearing!" he shouted, leaping for the nearest branch.

Scrambling down the tree, Sascha's shoes and gloves now gave her the advantage. She landed proudly in front of Tall William and his brother William the Almost Youngest. Her own brother was still half a tree behind.

She was about to brag about her victory when she spotted the stone elves hunkered amidst the vines and trees. There were at least ten statues in total, and they made for an eerie and unsettling sight, some with arms raised, swords at the ready; others frozen in midscream.

They were Nicholas St. North's band of outlaws, turned to stone by the Spirit of the Forest. The Spirit had spared North for he alone was true of heart. Rejecting her offer of riches, he had gone to the village's rescue when Pitch attacked again. He then decided to stay in Santoff Claussen, and became their wizard Ombric Shalazar's apprentice.

The Spirit of the Forest was just one of the magical barriers their wizard had devised to protect the village when he first created it. He'd also conjured up a hundred-foot-tall hedge, the great black bear the size of a house, and the majestic oaks that blocked the advance of anyone who tried to enter Santoff Claussen with ill intent. But none of these had been able to protect the children from the shadows and Fearlings at Pitch's command.

Petter and his friend Fog began crossing stick

swords with each other, acting out the battle that took place when Nicholas St. North had come face-to-face with Pitch.

Everything they knew and loved had seemed lost until North had galloped up to the rescue on Petrov. Though badly wounded, North had been able to drive Pitch away, but the children all worried that the Nightmare King would return. At this very moment Ombric, North, and their friend Katherine were far from Santoff Claussen, searching for the weapon—some sort of relic!—that would conquer Pitch forever.

The youngest William was near tears. "I'm afraid. Pitch told us he would come back."

"North, Ombric, and Katherine will find a way to stop him," Petter told him reassuringly.

William the Absolute Youngest wasn't entirely

convinced. "But Pitch's magic is strong. What if it's stronger than Ombric's?"

"What does Ombric always say?" Petter asked.

The youngest William thought for a moment, then his eyes grew bright. "Magic's real power is in believing," he proclaimed, clearly pleased to remember Ombric's very first lesson.

And he began to chant. "I believe! I believe! I believe!"

Sascha joined in. "I believe! I believe! I believe Katherine and North and Ombric will come home!"

CHAPTER TWO

In Which Old Friends Are Reunited

WHILE WILLIAM THE ABSOLUTE Youngest and Sascha chanted, the light around the children began to glisten and shine. The Spirit of the Forest was coming! In a whirl of shimmering veils laced with tiny gemstones, she appeared before them.

"Time for lessons," she whispered, her soothing voice cheering the children as always. And her luminous, otherworldly beauty banished all worries. "Today you have a special surprise."

Lessons in Santoff Claussen were always a surprise. On any given day the children might learn how to build a bridge to the clouds or how to make rain come from a river rock. So if the Spirit of the Forest said the surprise was special, it must be amazing indeed.

The children broke into a run toward the village, with Petrov and the bear galloping beside them. The Spirit of the Forest glided above them, enveloping the children with trails of light that tickled and swirled around them. They paused only to stomp on the rift in the ground where Pitch had disappeared when he'd retreated. William the Absolute Youngest stomped the hardest of all.

Lessons took place inside Ombric's home in Big Root, the oldest tree in the village and the center of its magic. The huge branches swayed and waved as the children dashed up its massive roots and into its hollow. Ever since Ombric had set off on his mission with North and Katherine, the children's parents had been helping them with their lessons. But on this day, there was a surprise indeed. A towering stack of packages—all identical—cluttered Ombric's library. There were so many that the bees, spiders, and ants who kept Ombric's workroom tidy couldn't keep up with them.

In charge of the library was Mr. Qwerty, a glowworm who loved books above all other things. He could generally be found meandering up the spine of one book or down another, cleaning the covers or repairing torn pages. Roughly six inches long, he was a bright, springlike shade of green; had quite a number of legs; and wore small, round glasses perched on his nose. He was also the ultimate authority when Ombric was away.

He had wriggled down from the book stacks to oversee the package deliveries.

"Careful, now," he told them in a surprisingly humanlike voice. He was the only insect in the known world who spoke human languages.

Of course the children examined the presents with keen interest. "They look like North's work," said Fog.

The comment caused a wave of excited chatter. Then they noticed a small army of ants hauling a package larger than the others through Big Root's entrance.

"I wonder who *that* one is for," said William the Absolute Youngest, a hint of hopefulness in his voice.

"Are there any labels?" Sascha asked.

Just then the giant globe in the center of the room—the one that Ombric slept in—swung open. The inside was hollow except for a single wooden rod near the bottom, which Ombric stood on to sleep. The children always wondered how he managed to not

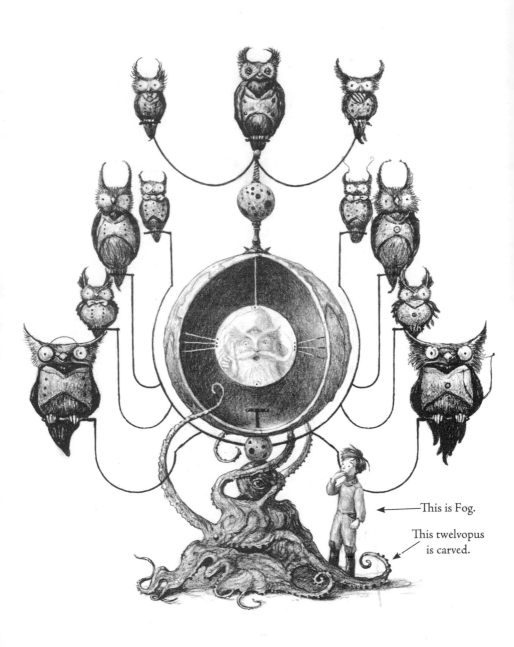

This is Fog.

This twelvopus
is carved.

fall off, but apparently for wizards, this was normal. As always, the dozen or so owls sat on their perches around the globe. They had the singular ability to communicate with the wizard with their minds.

The owls spent a good portion of their day preening, but now they began to hoot, slowly and deeply. At the center of the globe, a flat, circular glass plate appeared and started to glow. An illuminated image shimmered across it, and a familiar face came into focus. The children cried out happily. Ombric! It was Ombric! It had been weeks and weeks since he'd left, and questions tumbled out in shouts. "Where are you?" and "How is Katherine?" and especially, "Whose presents are these?"

The old wizard held up his hands. "First things first," he said with a laugh. "Tell me, has anyone had a nightmare?"

The children looked from one to the other, shaking their heads.

"No," said Fog.

"Old William had his birthday," Petter added.

"So did William the Absolute Youngest," Sascha reported.

"We're still the youngest and the oldest in the village," the youngest William piped up. "Even when I have a birthday, I'm still the littlest," he concluded with a frown.

"Then everything is as it was and as it should be," Ombric said with a satisfied nod. "I knew everything would be in order in the capable hands of Mr. Qwerty."

Upon hearing Ombric mention his name, Mr. Qwerty momentarily stopped resewing the binding of *Interesting Unexplainables of Atlantis, Volume 8*, and gave them all a little wave.

"Tall William," Ombric said, nodding at the boy. "I do believe you've gotten seven-eighths of an inch taller."

Tall William sat up a little straighter, a pleased smile on his face.

"Sascha, I hear you've figured out how to climb trees faster than a squirrel."

Sascha raised her feet and hands so that Ombric could see her invention.

"Ingenious," he said, stroking his beard. For every child, he had a cheering observation or a bit of praise or encouragement. Finally, he reached William the Absolute Youngest, who only wanted to know about the mysterious boxes.

Ombric could tell it was taking every ounce of the boy's self-control to not snatch one up. "To answer *your* question, young William, these boxes are presents from North. There is one for each of you. Each is exactly the same . . . until you pick it up," he said mysteriously.

"Since I'm the smallest, may I have the largest box?" asked the youngest William in his sweetest voice.

"*That* gift is special," said Ombric. "It's for all of you and should be opened last."

So each child chose one of the other boxes. Petter hefted one in his hand. It was surprisingly light.

Ombric smiled. "Now, think of a thing you would like, and it will be yours."

Petter closed his eyes and thought his very hardest. When he opened them, instead of a box in his hands, there was a pair of special shoes that would allow him to glide over water.

William the Absolute Youngest found a small mechanical soldier that could move about on its own.

It carried two swords, which it waved wildly. "It's just as I daydreamed," the youngest William cried. "Tell North thanks!"

There were even presents for Petrov (a carrot that would last a week) and the bear (an elegant ring for the paw that had been hurt in the battle with Pitch).

When all the wishes had been granted, the children turned to the larger box.

"That one is from Katherine," Ombric told them.

The ants carried the oversized package to Ombric's cluttered desk. As they set it down, the package began to unfold on its own, and out came a book.

"Katherine has written a story about our adventures since we left you. She misses you all and wishes she could tell you in person, but until then, her book will tell you the story. Now, before we start, we must begin with the first spell I ever taught you. Do you remember?" Ombric asked.

The children glanced at one another, grinning. Did they remember? Why, Sascha and the youngest William had just said that spell in the forest. Pleased to be a step ahead of their teacher for once, they began to murmur.

And as the words "I believe, I believe, I believe" filled the air, the green leather cover of Katherine's book opened with the contented sigh of a brand-new story entering the world. The pages turned, stopping to reveal a delicate drawing of Katherine. A gold ribbon marked the page. At the top, in Katherine's crisp handwriting, were the words "The Beginning."

CHAPTER THREE

Katherine's Story of Their Recent Amazements

To THE CHILDREN'S SURPRISE, the drawing of Katherine began to move and talk, and then her voice filled the room. The insects stopped their tidying, and the owls quieted their hooting. Mr. Qwerty paused in his work on the other books. The only other movement in Big Root came from the turning of the pages and the fluttering wings of the moths and butterflies that cooled the children against the summer heat. Standing watch outside, Petrov and the bear leaned forward to listen too, for even a horse and a bear love a good story.

"Did *you* also get a present?" William the Absolute Youngest asked the Katherine drawing. "If you didn't, I'll share mine with you when you get home."

"I got a wonderful present," Katherine assured him. "It's all a part of the story." And so she began, the pages of the book turning as she talked.

"Do you remember how Pitch disappeared into the ground to escape the sunlight?"

The children all nodded. Light was the one thing that Pitch could not stand.

"And remember how North made the mechanical djinni?"

The children nodded again.

"Good. Now I will tell you what became of the djinni."

The children leaned in closer, unable to take their eyes from the drawings as Katherine filled them in on what had happened over the last several weeks. "Pitch had possessed the djinni, disguised as a spider, and he had learned Ombric's spells of enslavement. He'd turned Ombric and North into porcelain toys and was going to destroy them. But the spectral boy named Nightlight saved us all."

The children gasped at this news. Petrov whinnied. Even the butterflies stopped fluttering.

"Nightlight is a great hero," Katherine said, her face beaming. "He was once the protector of the Man in the Moon, and he kept Pitch trapped for centuries! He is fearless and powerful, and now he's *our* friend and protector."

The children looked at one another, eyes wide.

"Nightlight and I found Ombric and North in the high Himalayas—the tallest mountains in the world. But since Pitch had gotten inside the djinni's metal shell, no light could get through to him, and he was practically invincible. He'd gathered a huge army of Fearlings, there was a terrible battle, and all hope seemed lost. Then—then!—Nightlight brought his own army to help us."

"What kind of army?" Petter had to ask.

Katherine grinned. "Moonbeams! And the Lunar Lamas sent Abominable Snowmen. You know, the ones Ombric has always talked about? They're real, as big as our bear, and there are hundreds of them. They're actually called Yetis."

The children cheered as Katherine's drawings showed scene after scene of the battle.

Then the pages paused at a sketch of Katherine, Ombric, and North as they stood within a sort of castle.

"Where is that?" Sascha asked.

"Ah! That is the Lunar Lamadary! It was built by the Lunar Lamas. They're holy men older than even Ombric."

The next drawing showed Ombric, North, and Katherine surrounded by Yetis and Lunar Lamas, then the page turned, and there was a drawing of the kindest-looking face they had ever seen.

"Who's *that?*" asked Fog.

"*He* is the Man in the Moon," Katherine told him. The children murmured amongst themselves. The Man in the Moon!

"The Man in the Moon told us Pitch had crashed to Earth, and it was Nightlight who'd trapped him, deep underground, for all of those centuries when he'd disappeared!" Katherine recounted. "The Man in the Moon told us that now that Pitch has returned, he will never stop, and he asked us if we would join the war to destroy Pitch forever."

"So there will be more battles?" William the Almost Youngest gulped.

"Does that mean we won't see you for a long time?" asked Fog.

"When are you coming home? We miss you," Sascha added.

The children's questions, and Katherine's answers, were drowned out by a loud honking noise.

Katherine began to laugh. "I'll tell you more later—I have my baby goose to take care of!"

A drawing of a very large gosling appeared on the page.

William the Absolute Youngest jumped closer for a better look. "Is that your present?"

"Yes! Her name is Kailash. She's a Himalayan Snow Goose, and she's going to grow as big as a horse. She thinks I'm her mother. But tonight at bedtime, my book will tell you all about her, I promise."

Then the book closed itself slowly, and the children were left with the impossible task of having to wait till bedtime to hear the rest of the story. Yet they were the children of Santoff Claussen! Mischief and magic would speed their day.

But, for a glowworm named Mr. Qwerty, there could not be enough time. Of all the books in Ombric's library, Katherine's was the most amazing. He would spend the rest of the day polishing it till it shined like a jewel.

CHAPTER FOUR

A Short Frolic Across the Planet

MEANWHILE, FAR AWAY IN the highest Himalayas, Katherine sat at one of the Moon-shaped tables in the library of the Lunar Lamadary. It was there that the Grand High Lama had taught her how to make her magic sketchbooks. How, if she thought hard enough, the drawings and the words she wrote could come to life on the page. The ink and paper she used were ordinary, but her mind, her imagination, was what gave the words and pictures their great power: the power to connect her to anyone who read her stories.

This was the first time she had tried to contact her

friends through one of these charmed books, and she was thrilled by how well it had worked. It was as if she were right there in Ombric's library, sitting next to the youngest William and the others. But it also made her miss her friends even more.

Nightlight sat perched on one of the library chairs, also listening to Katherine's story. He especially enjoyed the parts about himself. Katherine was never happier than when Nightlight was nearby. Though he never uttered a word, they had become very close. He was a miraculous friend. He could fly and speak to moonbeams with his mind. He made her laugh and always kept her safe. But it was in the nearly silent times that the real strength of their bond was evident. A friend who understands everything without being told is the rarest and best kind of friend. So this evening, without Katherine having to say a word,

Nightlight could tell that she missed the children back in Santoff Claussen and worried for their safety.

While Katherine fed her gosling—a process that involved several Yetis and an astonishing amount of oatmeal—Nightlight set off for Santoff Claussen to make sure that the children were safe. Katherine didn't see him leave, but she knew that he had left. This was the time of day when he would fly across the world to check for signs of Pitch.

Nightlight's life was divided into three parts: First was the time when he was guardian and protector of the little Man in the Moon, a time he could barely remember. He did not like to think about the second part—the long, dark years trapped in a cave with the Nightmare King, locked inside Pitch's cold heart. The third part of Nightlight's life was the present— the time of freedom and friendship. This part of his life was happier than any time he could remember. Whenever he leaped onto a breeze or a cloud or helped guard the children, he felt brave and strong and bright.

What made him happier still was Katherine. She was clever and kind and always ready to help her friends. And because Santoff Claussen was Katherine's home and was special to her, Nightlight checked the village extra carefully on his nightly patrols. If Pitch returned to hurt these people—Katherine's people—Nightlight would do everything in his power to stop him. Even at the risk of being imprisoned again inside Pitch's heart or, even worse, destroyed.

It was night when he arrived in Santoff Claussen. He scoured the forest, looking for danger. Was that the silhouette of a leaf in the moonlight—or the grasping fingers of a Fearling? Was it Pitch who momentarily blocked out the Moon—or a cloud drifting across the night sky?

After Nightlight had examined every out-of-the-way crook and corner of the forest and was assured that all was well, he moved on to the village. He peered into each cottage and yard. He even checked the layers of ground around Big Root. Finally, he held his moonlit staff over the dank, smoky scar in the dirt where Pitch had retreated. The moonbeam in his staff's diamond tip glowed brightly, and Nightlight was able to see that the scar looked just as it had the night before and the night before that. He checked a second time, just to be sure. But he saw no dastardly Fearlings disguised as shadows. No trace of Pitch anywhere.

On most nights this was enough to satisfy the

spectral boy. He would laugh his perfect laugh and hop onto the nearest cloud for a game of moonbeam tag. But tonight something felt wrong. Perhaps it was nothing, but all those years near Pitch had given him an instinct for evil. So he stayed back in the shadows, searching the sky as the children of Santoff Claussen made their way to Big Root for their bedtime story.

By now he knew their names: Sascha, Petter, Fog, all the Williams, and the others. He watched them secretly while they talked about the story Katherine would continue telling them tonight. As they hurried to prepare for bed, the Nightmare King was far from their minds. But as much as Nightlight loved Katherine's stories, he would be watchful. While the children gathered, his attention was in the shadows.

Pitch,
the Nightmare King

Fearlings

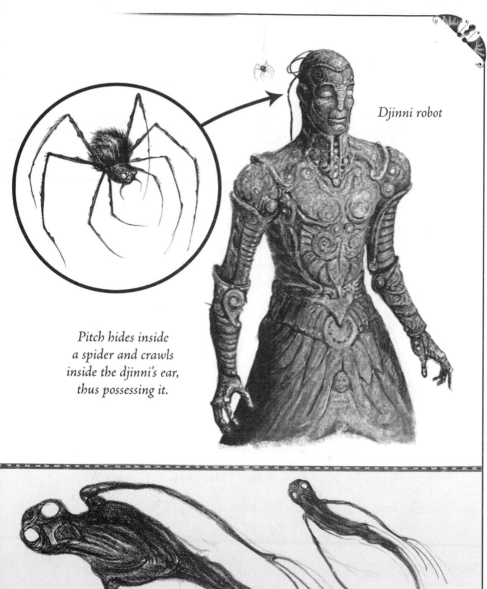

Djinni robot

Pitch hides inside a spider and crawls inside the djinni's ear, thus possessing it.

CHAPTER FIVE

A Bedtime Story with a Girl, a Goose, and Snowmen Who Are Not so Abominable

As THE CHILDREN OF Santoff Claussen tumbled into Big Root that evening, bunk beds materialized from the tree's hollow center. Each row, fanning out like the spokes of a giant wheel, was stacked five beds high. Twisting up and down the center was a spiral staircase.

William the Absolute Youngest scrambled up the stairs and was the first to reach his bed. He propped up his metal soldier against a pillow so he could see Katherine's book, which was suspended from the ceiling by a strand of Mr. Qwerty's silk. In another moment the rest of the children had found their bunks. Warm cocoa hovered in the air by each bed. Cookies also appeared. The children sipped and snacked and waited for Katherine's story to start again.

"She's going to tell us about the giant baby goose," Sascha said.

"And Nightlight," William the Absolute Youngest added. "He's my favorite!"

Nightlight, hovering outside, moved closer to the window at the sound of his name. Though worry still nagged at him, Petrov and the bear stood watch by the door, so Nightlight allowed himself to relax. He pressed his face against the glass, just in time to see Katherine's book reopen.

As it had that afternoon, Katherine's voice filled Big Root; the pages turned and the story started again. "Tonight I'm going to tell you about my gosling," Katherine's voice began. "The tale of the baby Snow Goose is sad—"

Sascha protested immediately. "I don't like sad stories."

"It only begins sadly," Katherine assured her.

Satisfied, Sascha leaned back against her pillow. A moth settled beside her, and together they watched the pages stop at a drawing of a giant pile of snow and ice.

"After the battle, Pitch had retreated inside the djinni's body," Katherine's drawing told them, "but as he left, he caused an avalanche that buried the nests of the Great Snow Geese."

The children oohed as the pages turned to a sketch of one of the enormous birds. Katherine explained how she helped them dig out a most beautiful silvery egg that had been buried in the snow. "The parents could not be found," Katherine said sadly, then she paused.

The children of Santoff Claussen all knew the story of Katherine's parents. They too had perished, in a blizzard when Katherine was just a baby, so it was no surprise to the children that Katherine's heart went out to the little orphaned gosling.

"We looked closer at the egg," Katherine told them. "It shuddered, and we heard a tiny tapping sound. A small hole appeared, then a little orange beak pecked through the eggshell, and then a white, feathered head pushed its way out!"

A picture of the baby goose half in and half out of the shell appeared before them.

"I wish you could feel how soft her feathers are. Maybe I'll be able to bring her home. I named her

Kailash—that's the name of the smallest mountain in the Himalayas."

"Kailash," repeated Sascha. "I like that name."

"Nightlight and I helped the geese rebuild their nests. They're enormous, nearly as big as a room. And the geese stand taller than North—and they are big enough for a person to ride upon!

"Ombric laughs every time he sees Kailash waddling behind me," Katherine continued. "I think he feels like a grandfather! We filled the nests with white goose down to make warm beds. Sometimes I even sleep with Kailash, so she won't feel lonely. But I'm very glad the Yetis know how to cook baby Snow Goose food."

Pictures of the giant hairy Yetis cooking for the gosling and of Kailash waddling behind Katherine made everyone laugh. Then more images followed as

Kailash comes into the world.

the book's pages turned: Katherine and Nightlight flapping their arms to try to teach the gosling to fly, and Kailash's first hops into the sky.

"Now she can fly for two or three hours at a time," Katherine announced proudly. "She's growing so fast, we have to keep making her nest bigger. She grows two or three inches a day."

A growth chart appeared, measuring Kailash against a wall.

"And I'm learning to speak Snow Goose. It's almost as hard as owl, but easier than eagle."

Now Fog sat forward. "Can Nightlight speak Snow Goose?" he asked.

Katherine answered, "He never says a word, but he seems to understand everything. With many creatures, I think he can talk just by thinking. But he likes to talk to me with pictures. Look!"

The children all leaned forward to see Nightlight's drawings, which were different from Katherine's—simpler and more childlike, but quite beautiful in their own way. There were sketches showing his old life in the Golden Age; pictures of the giant Lunar Moths, huge glowworms that lived on the Moon; the Man in the Moon when he was a baby; and the last battle of the Golden Age. There was also a darker picture of all those years Nightlight was trapped in a cave with Pitch. Finally, there was a picture of him being freed by his moonbeam friend, and then another of him saving the children of Santoff Claussen from the Fearlings that night in the forest.

Nightlight pressed his fingers against the glass. He loved seeing the children's reactions to his drawings.

"Yesterday morning Nightlight had a surprise

for me," Katherine said when the children settled back against their pillows. "I'd been waiting and waiting for Kailash to be big enough to ride, and secretly, Nightlight and Kailash had decided that it was the day! Kailash nudged my arm with her beak and lowered herself, so that I could climb onto her back.

"So I did. She unfolded her beautiful wings, and we took to the air. It felt as if we could fly forever. We flew all over the Himalayas, even the tallest mountain in the world, and of course we flew over the mountain Kailash was named for. We flew until it was dark. And then I tucked Kailash into her nest and told her a bedtime story about all of you till she fell asleep, and now it's time for all of us to do the same." The book began to close. "Good night, everyone. Dream of Kailash and me, and we will come home to see you soon."

The story had ended happily, as Katherine had promised.

William the Absolute Youngest yawned and rolled over with a quiet snore. Sascha kicked off her covers, and a troop of beetles pulled them back up over her shoulders. Petter was soon dreaming about giant geese and Abominable Snowmen.

Katherine hadn't told her friends that North and Ombric were trying to discover where the other relics from the Moon were hidden; she hadn't told them that the Nightmare King had vowed to turn her into a Fearling princess and to make nightmares real. Those things scared her and she knew they'd scare her friends too. Besides, she was sure Nightlight would be watching over them. Nightlight, who never slept and never dreamed, would keep nightmares, both imagined and real, away.

Petrov and the bear stood watch at Big Root's entrance while Nightlight sat just outside the window. His guard was up.

The night was too still. Something was wrong.

Something was coming.

CHAPTER SIX

Amazing Discoveries and Ancient Magic

WHILE KATHERINE WAS TELLING her bedtime story, North was studying the sword the Man in the Moon had bestowed upon him. He knew he was in a race against time. Pitch would return, and when he did, Nicholas St. North wanted to be ready. He prided himself on being the best swordsman in the world. Indeed, in his bandit days, he had once defeated an entire cavalry regiment with nothing more than a bent steak knife. But this sword was—blast it!—confounding.

Etched on its handle in a clear, handsome script

was the name TSAR LUNAR XI. The Man in the Moon's father had been the last tsar, or ruler, of the Golden Age, and his sword had been crafted with more care than even North himself was capable of. North had hammered out many a fine weapon, even some forged from bits of ancient meteor, but nothing like this amazing blade. It never seemed heavy, no matter how long North practiced with it. Its hilt closed tightly around his hand whenever he began to wield it, then loosened when he was ready to put it away. It could slice whole boulders in half with one slash. It wasn't a sword for slaying your average enemy, that was certain. But he wanted—needed—to understand all of its hidden powers. How else would he make the best use of it, especially against Pitch?

The Yetis did what they could to help. The crafty warriors possessed an amazing arsenal of arrow guns, pikes, bludgeons, spears, dirks, knucklers, and daggers, and they used all of them against this amazing sword. North was victorious every time, but it wasn't always his skill that won the day. It was the blade itself.

The sword had a mind of its own. It would leap from its sheath and into North's hand whenever there was danger—even during the friendly pretend attacks of the Yetis. It seemed to guide him to block an opponent's every thrust.

This piqued North's pride. The sounds of him yelling, "Quit that! I'm the best swordsman who ever breathed air!" and "Do what I say, you ancient pile of stardust!" could often be heard echoing through the Lamadary during sword practice.

That morning, in a practice battle with Yaloo, the fierce and friendly leader of the Yetis, North vanquished the hairy giant easily. And Yaloo carried the most feared of all Yeti weapons, an Abominable Mood Swing! Yaloo didn't seem to mind, but North was starting to feel sorry for him.

"You'll get me next time," North said with a good-natured chuckle. As he reached up to shake hands with Yaloo, the sword flew from his grasp. It appeared determined to fall from the tower.

North grabbed wildly for it, but it was too quick. He and Yaloo looked down in horror. Tashi, one of Yaloo's lieutenants, was just below, with the Grand High Lama. They were both standing on their heads meditating. The sword was heading straight for them.

What does one shout to a meditating Yeti and an ancient warrior Moon monk when a magic sword is about to impale them? North wondered fleetingly.

"Get off your heads before you lose 'em!" he bellowed.

Then a remarkable thing happened: As the weapon neared them, it stopped its fall. It hovered in the air for a moment, then began to rise. North reached out, his hand beginning to tingle. And even though the sword was a hundred feet below, it instantly flew back up to him and slapped into his palm with a satisfying *thwack*. Down below, Tashi and the Grand High Lama remained in their headstands, completely unaware of their near demise.

North turned the weapon over and over in wonder. The sword had fallen on purpose, to show him one of its secrets—that it could change direction to avoid causing harm. So he tried to test its sharpness with his thumb, but the sword's tip pulled away. "Can the sword wound only my enemies?" he asked out loud.

Yaloo motioned for him to try to slice him.

North paused, but Yaloo was adamant. So North took a breath and then slashed the blade directly toward Yaloo.

The Yeti didn't flinch, and once again the sword veered off, refusing to cause harm.

"The blasted thing. I expect a sword to do what I want. Why give me a weapon that fights *against* me?" North fumed.

The Yeti eyed North with an amused expression. "Perhaps the weapon is fighting *for* you," he suggested.

That pleased North. He was nodding in agreement when he heard a quiet "Ahem" behind him. North turned. Ombric stood there. He seemed eager to talk.

"I've been working on something that might help

us," the wizard said, as if picking up from a prior conversation—one that had nothing to do with North's sword.

North saw great excitement in the wizard's eyes. Ombric had already discovered that the Lamas had a magnificent clock that recorded every second of time. It was one of the few possessions the Lamas had been able to bring to Earth before Pitch had destroyed their home planet. They told Ombric the clock was as old as time itself, and it could send its user back a day, a year, or even an eon.

The wizard had been relentlessly studying the great, round clock. He couldn't believe that he—the prince of invention—had never tried to create such a marvel himself. The clock, more than thirty feet high, looked like nothing he had ever seen before. It was made up of dozens of interlocking rings that spun and rotated inside of one another. The rings were formed from a pale metal known only on the Lamas' home planet, and in the center stood a column of round clock faces of various sizes. These were used to set the clock to the exact time and place in history to which one wanted to journey.

With some trial and error, Ombric had learned how to go on short visits into the past.

No matter how much time he actually spent in the past, he returned to the present within minutes of when he left. Everyone in the Lamadary got used to seeing him pop up out of nowhere, with fantastic tales of his adventures.

One day he told Katherine he went to see the Great Pyramid of Giza being built. "Good thing they'd learned to levitate solid rock back then or they would never have finished the thing," the wizard declared. "Odd, though, that it was once topped with egg-shaped stone."

After another journey, he landed in the middle of the courtyard at the Lamadary, red-faced and panting, a large tear in his robe.

North had never seen the wizard so out of sorts. "What's wrong, old man?" he asked.

"Most dinosaurs are really very friendly creatures," Ombric answered once he caught his breath. "But those rex fellows, Tyrannosaurus? A bit snappy when hungry."

All of these journeys back and forth through time made for interesting stories, but North didn't see how they could help them defeat Pitch.

But this time Ombric planned to do more than merely go back in time. "I'm going to travel back to the moment when Pitch attacked the Moon," he told North. "I'll be able to see exactly where the relics fell. Finding them is our best hope of defeating him." And off he went.

But on this trip, something unusual—baffling, even—occurred. Ombric was very disturbed as he told them his latest adventure. They were eating supper in the busy dining hall of the Lamadary. Yetis, Lamas, and Snow Geese ate noisily as he related what had happened.

"I was back in time, just before the last battle of the Golden Age," he told them. "I could see Pitch's ship hiding on the dark side of Earth, lying in wait to attack the Moon. Suddenly, it occurred to me to warn the Man in the Moon and his family. I hoped to stop this whole history *before it could even begin*. But I sensed someone standing next to me.

"I turned to look, and there, to my utter amazement, floating beside me, was a most curious fellow. He was at least seven feet tall, wearing robes of a most peculiar design, and holding a long staff with an egg-shaped jewel at one end."

"Who was he? Did he say anything?" asked Katherine.

"He did indeed," confirmed the wizard. "One word, which he repeated: 'Naughty. Naughty.'"

"Is that it?" North demanded, lowering his soup spoon.

"Not quite," explained Ombric. "He touched my shoulder with the jeweled egg, and I suddenly found myself back here!"

"You've told me of many strange things, Ombric, but this takes the soup," said North, sipping again at his dinner.

"I left out perhaps the strangest part," added the wizard ominously. "The fellow's ears . . ."

"Yes?" said North.

Ombric leaned forward. "Mr. North," he said with dramatic relish. "They were the ears of a gigantic rabbit."

CHAPTER SEVEN

A Tall Tale for a Rabbit

KATHERINE AND NORTH SIMPLY did not know what to say about a seven-foot-tall talking rabbit. They'd seen so many amazements with the great wizard, but this struck them as, well . . . outstandingly odd.

North was the first to voice his doubts. "An interstellar talking Rabbit Man?" he questioned. "Are you sure all this time travel isn't scrambling your brains?"

Ombric raised an eyebrow at his former pupil.

"It does sound, hmmm . . . very *unusual*," added Katherine.

Ombric's eyebrow rose even higher. He was stunned that they doubted him. His temper began to rise. Then his mustache began to twist into tight curls.

But then Ombric remembered that he, too, had doubted the existence of this rabbit when he'd first read about him in an ancient text from Atlantis. In fact, he'd discounted the creature as merely a myth until he saw it floating next to him.

"If I am not mistaken," began the wizard in his most patient teacher voice, "this Rabbit Man, as you call him, is a Pooka—the rarest and most mysterious creature in the universe."

North and Katherine were intrigued; it was their eyebrows that now rose.

"They are among the oldest creatures in creation," continued Ombric, "so little is known about them and even less understood. It is said that they oversee the health and well-being of planets."

"This Pooka is mysterious indeed," interrupted the Grand High Lama. He and the Lamas stood serenely in their usual V formation. They'd entered the room, as always, in complete silence and had startled our heroes with their arrival.

"You *know* him? It?" asked Ombric, visibly surprised.

"We know he is a him, not an it," replied a tallish Lama.

"We know he has a vast knowledge," said another.

"We know he is difficult to know," said the shortest.

"We know he prefers to be unknown," said one of the others.

"We've heard he likes eggs," said another.

". . . and chocolate," added the shortest one.

"We *think*," concluded the Grand High Lama.

Katherine, North, and Ombric mulled over that uncommonly informative aria of information from the Lamas.

"A robe-wearing Rabbit Man who time travels and likes eggs," summarized North, trying not to laugh.

"And chocolate!" said Katherine mischievously.

"A substance he apparently invented," interjected the Grand High Lama.

"I thought *I* invented chocolate!" said Ombric indignantly.

"That, my dear Ombric, is what the Pooka *wants* you to think," replied a Lama.

"We *think*," added another.

Ombric shook his head in confusion. "I'm going time traveling. At least the past is certain. That much I do know."

"But do not tamper with events in the past," warned the High Lama.

"It is forbidden," said the tallest Lama.

"And the Pooka will not like it," said another.

As the wizard entered the time machine and made his settings, he replied, "Good!" And vanished into the certainties of the past.

North and Katherine stared at the clock for a few moments, then shared a concerned glance.

"I always worry about him when he goes back there. Wherever 'there' is," North admitted.

Katherine gave a small nod. "Me too."

"But he's a tough old bird," North reasoned just as Kailash came waddling up and began nuzzling her head against them. "This tough young bird needs feeding," he chuckled.

He picked Katherine up and set her on Kailash's

back. "Your goose is as big as Petrov—and still growing!"

"Want to help me feed her?" asked Katherine.

"Maybe tonight. I've got to keep working," North told her, reaching up to brush her hair out of her face. Her hair was always falling over one eye, and North would often brush it back.

Katherine looked down at her dashing friend. She was a little worried about him too. He'd been working so hard, trying to figure out how to use the new magic sword.

"That's all right. Nightlight will help me," she assured him.

She thought back to the day she, North, and Ombric had bowed before the Man in the Moon, had pledged their oath to continue in the fight against Pitch. North had sworn to use his sword wisely and well. So study he must. She was grateful for Nightlight's help, for being a Guardian was harder than any of them had realized. And it was about to get harder than they'd ever imagined.

CHAPTER EIGHT

A Hop, Skip, and a Jump Through Time

DEEP INSIDE THE CLOCK, Ombric was somersaulting through time at a furious pace. The world around him flickered from day to night faster than the blink of an eye. He saw seasons pass in seconds. Centuries flew by as he drifted up and away from the Lamadary. He looked skyward as the sun and stars spiraled past him at rocket speed. Day. Night. Day. Night. Faster than could be said and in reverse. The Moon was there too, and in a flash he saw the explosion of Pitch's galleon and the last great battle of the Golden Age. But it all happened too fast. The relics fell from the Moon too quickly for him to track them.

Ombric wasn't worried. He would slow down his trajectory on the return trip and take note of their whereabouts. And if his plan worked, he wouldn't need to.

He began to drift away from Earth, going deeper and deeper into the vast dazzlements of space. He was traveling so swiftly through time that comets, planets, and galaxies pivoted and sparkled around him like fireworks, but their size was beyond description.

Then Ombric realized that the flashes he was seeing were the deaths of the Golden Age worlds. What he was watching was Pitch's galleon destroying one Constellation after another. Then, as Ombric continued to pinwheel backward through time, the universe around him brightened.

Golden Age ships coursed through the sky around

him. This was it! The age he had studied for so long but never dreamed he would see. He could barely take it all in. The cities he saw were colossal, magnificent, more magical than anything he had ever imagined. It broke his heart to think of the vanished wonder and glory of this perfect era, and he became more determined than ever to implement his plan.

He soon found himself at the infamous prison planet, the huge rusted dungeon where the Fearlings had been locked after the Golden Age Armies had captured them. As time slowed down, he stopped his journey just moments before Pitch was overtaken and the Fearlings had escaped. Ombric hid behind a large pillar an arm's length away from Pitch, who was standing in a guard's station in front of the prison's only door.

It was remarkable to see his nemesis as he had been before his change to evil. He looked every inch a great hero. Stalwart. Valiant. Even noble in his Golden Age military uniform. But his determined expression was weary and tinged with sorrow.

From behind the massive door, Ombric could hear a drone of whispers and mutterings from the prisoners. The noise would rise to a crescendo, then sink low, pulsing eerily from within.

What an awful sound, thought Ombric. *It's like evil itself. To hear that day after day would drive any man insane.* And indeed, the ghostly noise seemed to weigh on Pitch. His face was drawn, his fists clenched in anxiety.

But then he pulled a silver locket from his tunic pocket; the chain hung around his neck. He tapped the clasp and it swung open, revealing a small photograph. Ombric could just make out the face of a little girl. Pitch stared at the image, seeming to take great solace in the picture. His face softened and his

sadness eased. Ombric knew that expression. He'd seen it countless times. It was the look of a father gazing at his child. *Pitch had a daughter!* The wizard could feel Pitch's longing to see his child in person.

The Fearlings sensed his longing too. Their strange mutterings shifted in tone, their pleadings took on the voice of a small girl. "Please, Daddy," they whispered. "Please, please, please open the door."

A momentary spark of hope crossed Pitch's face. His eyes lit up, and then they dimmed as he recognized the sound for what it was: a Fearling trick. He visibly steeled himself against the evil, bracing his shoulders, clenching his jaw, but the Fearlings started to beg again.

"Daddy," they cried. "I'm trapped in here with these shadows, and I'm scared. Please open the door. Help me, Daddy, please."

Pitch looked again at the photograph. The

pleading grew more desperate. More hypnotic. Pitch seemed to be slipping into a trance.

Suddenly, his face grew wild with panic. He reached for the door. The locket fell from his neck. Ombric caught it in midair and was about to block Pitch from opening the prison door when the mysterious Pooka reappeared. Ombric found he could neither move nor utter a sound.

The Pooka held up his hand and shook his head. "That's a no-no," he scolded.

The Lamas had told Ombric he could not change events in his journeys through time, he could only observe them. The Pooka, it seemed, was there to stop his trying.

Ombric looked from the Pooka back to Pitch in time to witness agony and shock in the jailer's eyes— the desperation of a loving father trying to save his daughter from the Fearlings. As the door swung open, all that was visible was a roiling mass of dark, serpent-like creatures. Of course Pitch's daughter was not there. Before Pitch could even scream her name, he was surrounded by malevolent shadows. In less than an instant, they poured over, around, *into* him! It was a horrifying sight. One that Ombric would never forget.

Pitch struggled valiantly, but he soon succumbed to the evil flooding him, twisting him into a madman. He swelled to ten times his normal size; his face became monstrous and cruel.

As Ombric stared, transfixed, he felt the familiar touch of the Pooka's egg-tipped staff on his shoulder. He was being sent back to the present again. But as he began to dim and vanish, he saw Pitch throw his head back and roar with the menacing laughter of ten thousand Fearlings.

CHAPTER NINE

The Secret of the Sword

WHILE OMBRIC WAS WATCHING history unfold, North was in the Lamadary library studying the new sword. He'd examined it for weeks with all the methods at his disposal: magnifying glasses of every shape, size, and purpose. Microscopes, maxiscopes, telescopes. He'd come to so many mystifying discoveries, it boggled his agile mind. The metal of the sword could change itself. Sometimes it was mostly iron, then it shifted to steel, then to metals that North couldn't even classify. It could become highly magnetic or immeasurably strong, and at times it could emit various kinds of light. Sunlight. Moonlight. Comet light. Lights that had no name. North began to realize that the weapon was indeed a living thing.

In battle it would transform into a conventional sword—a long blade with a protective covering over the handle. But depending on the circumstances, it would sprout various mechanical additions. In darkness, for instance, a curious light-emitting orb would appear. When danger was imminent, the jewels on the hand guard would glow red. And at other times the hand guard itself would change, sometimes revealing maps of the stars or the Moon or the Earth itself.

But the how, why, and what of these gadgets were still a mystery to him.

North thought about what Ombric always said about magic—that its real power was in belief. North knew for certain that this sword had powers beyond explanation. The sword, he hoped, could tell him what he most needed to know. So he closed his eyes and concentrated on that belief with all his mind and heart. "I believe. I believe. I believe," he said very quietly. As he chanted the phrase over and over, his thoughts began to grow uncluttered, pure, sharp, until he had only one question. Where were the other relics? It was as if the sword now guided his mind.

And then, with the subtlest of clicks, North felt the sword change.

He opened his eyes to see that a metal orb had appeared. It opened, unwrapping like an intricate puzzle. Inside was a map of the Earth, and on the map were four glittering jewels. *Four jewels*—North's mind raced—*four jewels. . . . Were they the four relics?* That had to be it! Each jewel marked their position. They simply had to follow this map!

Eager to share the news with the wizard, North raced through the Lamadary, finding Ombric in the tower just as he was reappearing from his latest time travel.

"I have the answer, old man!" North cried, slapping him on the back.

"And I have new questions," said Ombric wearily.

At that moment Katherine ran into the room.

"Nightlight is missing!" she shouted.

CHAPTER TEN

Revelations, Terror, and Daring Deeds

KATHERINE TRIED TO REIN in her panic, but her quivering voice betrayed her. "He hasn't returned since last night. No one has seen him," she explained in a rush.

Both Ombric and North tensed. They knew that Nightlight's visits were as regular as clockwork. They also knew that Santoff Claussen was always his last stop before he returned to the Lamadary.

"Only one thing could delay the lad," said North, his voice low.

"Pitch," whispered Katherine.

Even as they spoke, Ombric was already trying to contact his owls. They were constantly on watch in his library and forever at the ready to report to him telepathically. He concentrated with all his might, but the line of mental communication was severed. How could that be? He could not sense even an echo of emotion from the owls. If they could not speak to him, he should at least be able to *feel* them. Especially if they were in danger or afraid. But there was nothing.

It was this nothingness that frightened him most. He spun around and caught North's eye. He didn't need to say a word—North understood immediately.

"To Santoff Claussen?" North asked.

"And right speedily" came Ombric's answer.

The question was, which method would get them there "right speedily"? Ombric knew he didn't have the stamina for astral projection[1]—time travel always

---

[1] *Astral projection: When you mentally project yourself from one place to another. It is also an ancient method of mystical travel. Only the most brilliant and daring are able to astrally project themselves.*

left him exhausted. Besides, North and Katherine couldn't join him in that mode. The reindeer? They needed the spectral boy to create the highways of light upon which they flew. The djinni, of course, was gone. Ombric's mind was anxiously calculating all the possibilities when he was interrupted by the sudden appearance of the Lamas.

"We have adequate conveyance," said the Grand High Lama.

"It is swift," said another Lama.

"And comfortable," added a third.

"And easy to pilot," agreed a shortish one.

Ombric dreaded the series of answers his next question would cause; the Lamas answered questions only in fragments.

"Where is the craft?" Ombric tried to sound patient and urgent at the same time.

The Lamas looked at one another, deciding who would answer first.

Ombric, North, and Katherine shifted impatiently. Time was wasting.

Finally, the Grand High Lama spoke. "The craft? Why, you stand within it," he said with stunning simplicity. "You need merely to say where you'd like to go, and this tower will rocket you there with both speed and accuracy." Then the Lamas began to shuffle silently toward the courtyard.

"We are certain you can handle the situation," said the Grand High Lama as they reached the arching doorway.

"But we suggest you sit down for the trip," said the tallest.

"The trajectory is most speedy," said the shortest.

"At least when last we used it," said another.

"Thirty thousand years ago," added the Grand Lama as he exited last.

North, Ombric, and Katherine looked quizzically at one another. They each took to a chair and then glanced up at the glass-topped ceiling of the tower. It was perfect for observing a journey.

"We have all we need, I think," said North, gripping his sword.

Katherine suppressed a smile. She knew Kailash,

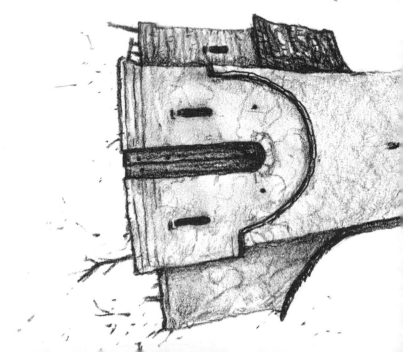

asleep under a nearby table, was aboard for the trip. But she thought it best to keep that to herself.

Ombric turned to her. "My dear, give the order."

She grasped the arms of her chair tightly. "To Santoff Claussen as fast as—"

But before she could finish the sentence, they were already blasting off.

The Lamadary Tower is a swell way to travel.

CHAPTER ELEVEN

As the Tower Flies

THE LAMAS WERE TRUE to their word. The tower was a marvelous airship. No sooner had they taken off than the entire interior began to mechanically transform. As the tower shifted horizontally in its trajectory, their chairs glided toward the glass ceiling. The floor began to pivot and lean, as did the walls, until they formed a sort of ship's cabin with large Moon-shaped windows.

The woodwork, the mosaic floor tiles, the wallpaper, the instrument panels—every aspect of the cabin took on different shapes of the Moon: full or half or crescent. It was enchanting and, as promised, comfortable.

North examined all the charts and instruments carefully. "This screen shows our present position," he determined, then pointed to another and another. "This one our speed. This one our route. This one our time of arrival."

He seemed pleased by the instruments' reading. "We should be there within the hour," he told them.

Katherine was relieved to hear North's prediction. To travel from the Himalayas to the farthest corner of eastern Siberia in a matter of minutes was an astounding thing. Even the reindeer had not been able to achieve that kind of speed.

But Ombric was quiet. Katherine could tell from his expression that even this was not fast enough. Then she saw the locket he clutched in his hand.

"What's that?" she asked. Ombric was lost in thought and didn't seem to hear her. She gently took the locket from him and opened it to see the picture of the young girl, who was close to her own age. Katherine looked intently at the lovely girl with raven-black hair and haunting eyes.

"She's Pitch's daughter," said Ombric, his own eyes closing as he tried in vain to reach the owls. "I saw him holding it, back in time, before he became evil."

Katherine was amazed. She had no memory of her own father. And though she tried to imagine what he looked like, the image in her mind was never very clear—she'd been too young when she had lost him. It was equally difficult to imagine Pitch ever being a father. Or that he had ever been good. She remembered with a shudder that Pitch had vowed to turn her into a Fearling princess. But mixed with that feeling of dread was now a sadness that twined with her own sense of loss and longing.

Pitch had a daughter. What had happened to her?

And what had happened to Nightlight?

Kailash had found her way from the back of the tower. She honked and struggled to squeeze through the door of the main cabin, and with one great shove, she made it. She snuggled next to Katherine, her long neck twisting around her protectively, her feathered body a warm brace to lean against.

North looked at Katherine's sorrow-filled face. He was glad that Kailash was there to comfort her. He knew from Ombric's concentrated silence that things in Santoff Claussen would be perilous.

So he steadied himself for the darkness that lay ahead.

CHAPTER TWELVE

Delicate Darkness

BEFORE THE TRAVELERS KNEW it, their craft started dropping in elevation, flying lower and lower, until it was practically skimming the treetops of Santoff Claussen's enchanted forest. They had to squint to see the village. Clouds blocked the Moon and the stars. More unsettling was that not a single light shined from any window. The village was a shadow.

The airship landed with surprising silence at the edge of the forest. North carefully opened the Moon-shaped door, and they all gazed out on their village. It had never been this quiet. North looked to Ombric with a tense, questioning expression, then unsheathed the magic sword and climbed out first. "Stay behind me. Run if I say so," he told Katherine. The sword was transforming itself as he spoke, its light emerging magically from the blade. The glow lit their way. North sensed a vibration—was the sword signaling danger? He was not sure.

They walked toward Big Root slowly, scanning the mournful landscape for any signs of life.

Katherine had never seen a night so black or heard a silence so quiet—not even on the night when Pitch had first found her and her friends in the forest. It was as if all the life of the place had gone away. There was no movement. No breeze. Not one firefly or night bird flew to greet them. Even the raccoons and the badgers were nowhere to be seen.

Katherine reached for North's hand and kept the other on Kailash's neck. "Where is everyone?" she whispered.

Instead of answering her, Ombric stopped short. Something was glinting in the light from North's sword. Ombric stooped to pick up what appeared to be a small piece of glass. He held it up to the light: It was a tiny porcelain squirrel. It was like a toy. Turning it this way and that, he said, "It appears that Pitch has further mastered the spells of enslavement." He looked troubled and began to walk forward again, his eyes continuing to search the ground.

Though the eerie quiet persisted, the thick cloud cover began to dissipate as the threesome made their way into the village, so at least some moonlight began to penetrate the gloom. But this simply allowed them to better see the horror all around them.

In every direction, Katherine saw small porcelain versions of living things. Whole platoons of squirrels, raccoons, and foxes all looked to be frozen in mid-battle.

Try as she might, Katherine couldn't keep the tears back. Had Pitch frozen everything? She nearly stumbled over the Spirit of the Forest. The Spirit's normally flowing veils hung still and stiff, her gemstones were dulled with the lifeless shine of ceramics. Her frozen expression was one of fierce determination. In her hands she clasped a jeweled sword. She had clearly been petrified at a moment of intense struggle, just as she had once done to all who had fallen under her spell.

Katherine peered into the Spirit's glassy eyes and noticed something she had never expected to see there: fear. Then Katherine wiped her tears and willed herself to shed no more; she needed to keep alert. She jogged to catch up with North and Ombric.

North was barreling ahead. Katherine desperately hoped to find that at least one living thing had escaped Pitch's enslavement spell, but when they neared the village and Big Root, she realized that that was not to be. Every breathing creature in Santoff Claussen had been turned into a china doll. Even the bear. Again Katherine had to fight back tears. The bear looked so small and helpless now.

North's horse, Petrov, was lying on his side in front of Big Root's shattered door. He looked as if he had been on his hind legs in the midst of kicking the shadows away when he'd been overwhelmed by Pitch's spell. North ran to him, speechless.

Ombric walked among the parents of the children. They lay surrounding the tree, frozen, terrified expressions marring their faces. His fears turned to outrage as he swept into Big Root itself. The owls sat immobile on their perches around Ombric's globe. The dozens of honeybees and ants that resided in Big Root lay scattered on the floor like tiny china game pieces tossed aside by an unruly child.

Ombric and North surveyed the damage in stunned silence. The library was stripped bare. Not a single book remained. The beakers and test tubes Ombric used for his magical experiments had been dashed to the ground.

"No books and no children," Ombric said quietly. "And where is Mr. Qwerty?"

Katherine came up behind him. Where was Petter? Sascha? All the Williams? She sank to her knees, carefully brushing her insect friends to one side so they wouldn't be stepped on. Then one glittering piece of crystal caught her eye. She reached for it. Only then did she notice a sliver of a blade nearby. Then another. And another.

Her hand shook as she examined the pieces. Glistening drops, like beads of light, surrounded them. "It's the tip of Nightlight's staff," she gasped.

Ombric and North crouched beside Katherine. A small tarnished moonbeam—Nightlight's moonbeam!—was hidden beneath the largest piece of the shattered blade. With great care, Katherine cupped the beam into her hands.

"What happened, moonbeam?" she asked gently. "Where is everyone?"

Only Ombric spoke moonbeam, so he waved his staff and suddenly the little fellow's memories were displayed on the round glass of the globe bed.

The moonbeam shimmered with all the strength it could muster, and though it wavered and flickered, Ombric, North, and Katherine could see and hear the terrible story of Pitch's return.

CHAPTER THIRTEEN

The Moonbeam Tells His Tale of Woe

WE ARE IN THE Big Root tree, began the moon-beam, on the limbs outside a window. We watch the children in their beds. The Katherine book is telling stories of the Kailash. All warm and happy the children are! And so are we, my Nightlight boy and I. But we feel something that is a bother to us. A Pitch kind of scariness. It comes like a wind. We cannot see it. But we are feeling it. The clouds come dark and quick, and the moonlight and the stars are gone all suddenly. So my Nightlight boy looks out to the forest. All around is a badly sound. The forest creatures from every side are a-chatter and screamly.

So fiercely fast the shadows come. Out of the forest. Toward the village. Toward the Big Root. Toward *us*! The Forest Spirit lady, she is fighting most ferocious, but the Pitch cannot be stopped. He wears the metal djinni suit and has a sword so dark. It takes all light that comes near. The Pitch says words— spells, I thinks—and all who are close go changed. They're made small and still, and they move no more.

My Nightlight boy, his face is wild. He has the look of a knowing plan. This look I seen whenever he is about to do a deed most smart and daring.

So I listens as he tells me with his thinking talk: *The game I try will be most tricky. Don't be fooled by what you see.*

Then he looks close at me and says fiercely strong, *Fly straight and true and never fear.*

Then he takes the staff on which I am tied and points me at the Pitch. He throws me with all his mights. So fast I go. Fast as light. And into the metal I hits. The diamond dagger in which I live goes quick through the metal of the djinni armor and into the darkness of the Pitch himself. I hear the Pitch make a moan of deepest hurt, and I feel him fall. But I can see the cold black heart of him. I have not pierced it. All around me is the darkness. The cold heart still beats.

The Pitch, he is moving, I can tell. But what is happening outside I cannot see. I hear many shouts and screams most loud. I hear the bear a-roaring and the horse make his battle sounds, but one by one, they all go quietlike.

I hear the Pitch.

He breathes hard and heavy, but he is a-shouting

now. "WHERE IS IT! TELL ME!" he's asking most meanly.

Then he makes a groan sound, and I feel the pulling. Then I am out of the Pitch, but he is pointing *me*. Pointing me at my Nightlight boy. We are in the Ombric library, but there be no books. All are gone. The little wormly is gone. Just my Nightlight boy and the childrens. He is a-front the childrens, as if to protect them, but he is much hurt. On his knees from the hurt. But his face is not fearish. Neither are the children's. And this makes the Pitch anger get bad. Very bad.

So he's a-shouting, "I WANT THE BOOKS! THE BOOKS OF SPELLS!" Not any of the Williams or the Petter boy or the Sascha girl tells a word. Fearlings, they are all around the room now. Coming closer, closer to my Nightlight boy and the childrens.

But my Nightlight boy says loud and clear, "We fear you none!" I've never heard him speak with his voice. It is a magic voice he has. Like faraway memories and echoes of long ago. Then he laughs at the Pitch and leaps to attack. But the Pitch throws me and the staff at my Nightlight boy, and then all around is strangeness. The diamond tip hits my boy! And there's lights and shatterings. The diamond, it did not pierce my boy, but it is brokened into many pieces. And my boy lays still. On the ground! He shines not bright, but dim and flickering.

My broken dagger has let me loose. I am free. So I goes to my boy, but the Pitch hits me with his dark sword and it hurts me. Takes some of my light. So I am weak-feeling and cannot help my boy. The childrens look a little feared, but they muster strong and stare angry at the Pitch and his Fearlings.

"I need those books!" says the Pitch, all quiet and scary. "Ombric must give them to me. So you little ones will be my bait!" Then he opens his dark cape. It seems to eat the light as it wraps around the room. In a blink all is gone. The Fearlings gone. The childrens gone. My Nightlight boy gone too. And the Pitch.

Just me left. And the toy-turned owls.

Then the moonbeam turned to Ombric and the others. The childrens need us! My Nightlight boy said his game was most tricky and to never fear. I am trying. I hates the feeling I am having. A scaredy feeling. But I am stronger by the telling of the tale!

CHAPTER FOURTEEN

A Moonbeam, a Mystery, and a Muddle

MOONBEAM WAS EXHAUSTED AND dimmed again as he lay in Katherine's palm.

Ombric, North, and Katherine were each trying to make sense of everything the moonbeam had told them. They knew the situation was dire, but they kept surprisingly calm. They had been growing increasingly confident since taking the Man in the Moon's oath. And now the three began to work almost as one, as one mind. Ombric had read that friendship could produce a sort of magic. North was new to the concept, but he was keenly aware of its possibilities, and Katherine, the youngest, was, in this case, the wisest. She knew in her bones that friendship was a magic with powers beyond words or possibilities. And so the magic grew stronger. They could feel one another's thoughts coming together, sorting through the various threads of what the moonbeam had reported. Discovering questions. Searching together for answers. This curious union caught them completely off guard, especially Ombric. Never in his centuries of conjuring had he felt this sort of shared purpose. A mental mind melding of sorts, he mused. It was strange. Thrilling.

Katherine wondered the first question aloud. "Where has Pitch taken Nightlight and the children?"

"What is this new sword he wields that can devour light?" North asked next. "And why the devil did Pitch want the library?"

"The diamond dagger was shattered!" Ombric declared. "All is strangeness."

The wizard's mind became totally focused as he tried to fathom the muddles and mysteries the moonbeam had presented to them. His mustache and beard began to twirl on their own at a lively pace. He felt Katherine and North connecting to his thoughts.

Ombric suddenly strode over to his empty bookshelves and began examining each intently. Only a few tiny scraps of paper remained, a bit from *Spells of the Ancient Egyptians,* another from *Interesting Unexplainables of Atlantis,* some tattered corners of random maps and charts. Even Katherine's storybook was missing. There was no denying it. The library Ombric had carefully amassed over hundreds of years had utterly disappeared.

Ombric closed his eyes and concentrated, casting about for remnants of leftover magic. "I find no evidence of a vanishing spell," he said, his voice edged with small relief. "No magic was used. The books still exist—somewhere." Then his eyes grew wide. The tips of his shoes stood on end. Katherine and North stared at him warily.

"He's taken them to the Earth's core!" Ombric proclaimed triumphantly. "That's where Pitch obtained the lead. His saber and cloak are made with it!"

North cocked his head. "Lead? What's so special about this lead?"

"Lead found at the core of Earth has been there since the planet was first formed," Ombric explained. "It has never known light—of any kind—so no light can penetrate it. It absorbs it. That's how Pitch was able to attack Nightlight and the moonbeam. He stole some of their light."

"The madman is growing more wily by the day!" North exclaimed. "And the library? Why was he after that?"

Ombric spoke more carefully, as if figuring it out as he went. "Pitch needs all the spells and enchantments in my volumes to become more powerful. To become, perhaps, invincible," he added with some measure of awe. "But, somehow, the library disappeared before he could get it." Ombric frowned. "And that's the part I can't make heads or tails of."

"Without magic, how can all those books just disappear?" North asked.

"Exactly!" said Ombric. "That's the puzzlement."

Katherine took in all of this new information. Her mind worked with lightning speed as she pieced together all the clues herself. What the moonbeam had told them, what they had found here, and what she thought it might all mean. Then suddenly she knew. "It's Nightlight!" she shouted. "He told the moonbeam not to believe everything it sees. He found a way!"

North and Ombric considered the idea, both becoming lost in thought. Then North's mustache began to twirl on its own, as Ombric's had moments before.

"If Pitch is at the planet's core, it's a trap!" North said, restraining his rage. "He knows we'll come to rescue the children." He drew his sword. "But he has not faced this blade since the Golden Age. And never with me at its command." He turned to Ombric. "How do we get to the Earth's core, old man?"

Ombric felt so proud of them. They were becoming a very potent and powerful team. But this elation gave way quickly to disappointment. He had no answer to the question. "*That* is a journey no man has ever made," he said with a furrowed brow.

Then North's sword began to glow and clatter. The cover of the blade's grip began to twist and unfold as it had before. One of its stones started to shine brightly.

All three of them peered at it. North's heart surged. "This is what I'd started to tell you about earlier, old man!" he cried. In a flurry of words he laid out what he'd discovered thus far of the sword's powers. "The sword is telling us where we must go. Where the next relic lies."

Ombric nodded sagely. His brows unfurrowed. He almost smiled. He *almost* began to laugh.

"What is it, old man?" asked North impatiently.

"Why, it's a map of Earth!" replied the wizard. "We must go to Easter Island!"

"Easter Island?" asked North.

"Yes! The legend says that's where the Pooka lives."

The trio began to think very hard.

Mustaches, beards, and eyebrows were twirling wildly on the men as they concentrated. As for Katherine, though she did not notice it, a single curl right in the middle of her forehead was twirling too.

CHAPTER FIFTEEN

Wherein the Friends Must Separate

KATHERINE SPOTTED PETROV AND the bear lying just outside Big Root's door and winced. They didn't look as though they were in pain, but still, it must be terrible to be unable to move or talk or even blink. "Can we unfreeze them now?" she asked Ombric. "Maybe they can tell us where the books are."

"I say we fly to the center of the Earth and rescue the children!" North blustered. Every muscle in his body strained to do something—anything—to help the children.

"How do you plan to do that?" Ombric asked,

folding his arms across his chest.

"I'll figure it out on the way," North said.

"Let's take things one at a time, shall we?" Ombric told him, looking around. "Perhaps Katherine is right, and the animals can tell us what became of my books. But an enslavement spell this powerful can't be reversed quickly. It needs to be done carefully and well." He shook his head. "It's the work of many, many hours."

"Then they'll have to stay like this until we return," North said to Ombric. "You can release them after we've crushed the Nightmare King. We'll help you."

Ombric tugged at his beard, frowning. "Some of these spells are trickier than others. If I wait too long, I fear this spell could be irreversible." He looked at the porcelain creatures scattered across his floor. "There are no two ways about it. I'll have to stay behind in

Santoff Claussen, and you'll have to continue on to Easter Island."

"Easter Island! We have to get to Pitch!" North bellowed.

Katherine added, "Nightlight is hurt!"

"The Pooka, if he can be found, will be able to lead you to the Earth's core," Ombric explained. "Pooka lore indicates that he has a series of tunnels that span the interior of the globe."

North began to object, but Ombric insisted. "By the time you reach Pitch, I expect to have restored our friends here and discovered the whereabouts of my library."

Looking up at him with her steady gaze, Katherine said, "You can do whatever you set your mind to."

Ombric raised an eyebrow. "The student reinterprets the teacher's lesson," he said. "Well done."

"Just do me a favor, old man," North conceded. "Release Petrov first. I can't stand to see him like this."

Ombric agreed. Then, with no time to lose, Katherine, Kailash, and North left Big Root.

On their way to the forest, Katherine looked into Old William's frozen eyes. "We'll be back," she promised him. "And so will all of your Williams."

She climbed into the air shuttle, strapped Kailash into a seat, and then did the same for herself.

"To Easter Island! Let's hope this Bunnymund creature actually exists," North said, scanning the sky for signs of trouble. "There's no setting for the Earth's core."

As he watched them rocket away, Ombric knew he could trust the brave girl he had raised and the young man who had been his apprentice. They would do what needed to be done.

CHAPTER SIXTEEN

The Curl Twirls

KATHERINE'S CURL BEGAN TO twirl again as she and North streaked toward Easter Island.

She did not like that they could not all stay together. But she was certain that Ombric was correct. Only he could manage the delicate and lengthy task of undoing all the enslavement spells that Pitch had conjured against Santoff Claussen. The parents, the owls, the insects, the Spirit of the Forest, the bear, Petrov—everything that breathed would have to be individually "un-toyed," as Katherine had termed it.

Still, she had been brave for so long, and truth be told, she was a little weary of having to be such a grown-up. She wanted Ombric near. He was like a father to her. And in times of danger, it feels good to have one's own father near, not thousands of miles away. But she bore this anxious feeling silently.

She knew they would need to be at their best, perhaps even more than their best, to save their friends and once again undo the dark plans of Pitch.

They were far above the ocean of the Pacific now. The Moon was clear and bright, and so close that they thought they could see the Man in the Moon and his Moonbots smiling down at them.

They rocketed forward—faster even than they had flown on their way to Santoff Claussen. And the stone on the magic sword that marked Easter Island blinked steadily.

Katherine looked at it with alarm. "Is that a bad sign?"

North shook his head. "Quite the opposite! It means we're getting closer."

Kailash honked. "She's glad," Katherine said.

"Of course she is; we're on the wildest goose chase in history!" North joked.

Katherine was glad for the joke, and even more glad to know that North sensed her worries and was trying to cheer her.

The dials of the airship let out an alarm. Up ahead was Easter Island! The sun was just beginning to rise when the ship settled gently on a sandy beach. It cast a soft glow over the island, and Katherine could hardly wait to get out. North opened the shuttle's door and climbed down the ladder.

Katherine patted her pocket to make sure she had

her dagger. Satisfied, she turned to Kailash. "Stay here until I know it's safe," she told the gosling, then she jumped onto the sand after North.

Together they began to explore the island.

Hundreds of giant stone heads sat ominously across the barren beach. Katherine had seen drawings of these colossal sculptures in Ombric's library. But they were much stranger than she'd expected and larger than she'd imagined.

North ran his hand across a mouth—a narrow slit below an enormous stone nose. "These were carved," he said. "But by who?"

There were no signs of life. No humans running over to see what had landed on their beach. No birds cawing in alarm. Katherine and North walked among the stone heads and wondered if there were any living creatures on the island at all. The only sound was that

of the waves coming in and going out again. Oddly, Katherine thought she smelled a hint of hot cocoa in the salty sea air. And she had the strangest sensation that they were being watched.

And they were! One of the stone heads had turned in their direction. Then another. And another. With the screech of stone scraping against stone, all the heads, as far as they could see, were slowly rotating toward them.

The orb on the magic sword was glowing even brighter. North took a chance. "Where can we find the Pooka?" he shouted out. "We need to get to the Earth's core—on the double!"

The heads didn't answer.

But as the echo of his shouts died away, something began to emerge from the top of each of the stone sculptures. Two stone shafts, almost like ears, slowly rose, stretching to sharp points at the tips. The heads had grown stone rabbit ears! Every one of them! Katherine and North exchanged uneasy glances.

Then something, or someone, twisted up out of the ground a dozen feet away, sending sand and grass flying in all directions.

Katherine and North found themselves looking at an extremely tall rabbit. He stood completely upright, not crouched like a bunny. He was at least seven feet tall (with ears) and wore green egg-shaped glasses and a thick green robe with golden egg-shaped buttons. Around his waist was a purple sash and waistcoat with egg-shaped pockets. He held a tall staff with an egg at its tip.

Katherine gave the Rabbit Man an uneasy smile.

The rabbit did not respond. He didn't even blink. In fact, he was so still that Katherine thought he might be a statue too. She took a step closer, but to her utter surprise, a group of armor-covered eggs with tiny arms and legs emerged from under the hem of the rabbit's robe. The eggs raised their bows. Their arrows, she noticed, had tiny egg-shaped points.

Katherine pulled back again, but North was less cautious. He had seen the rabbit's nose twitch and had an inkling.

"You are the Pooka, I presume?" he asked.

The rabbit became a sudden blur of motion. In less than a blink he was standing directly in front of them.

"I am E. Aster Bunnymund," he said in a deep, melodious voice. "I've been expecting you."

E. Aster Bunnymund,
last of the Pookas

CHAPTER SEVENTEEN

In Which Pitch Appreciates North's Ingenuity but Proves to Be a Dark Customer Indeed

NORTH'S MECHANICAL DJINNI WAS a truly inspired invention. Pitch took delight not only in the theft of his enemy's creation, but also in the wonderful things it could do. When he was inside the djinni, Pitch could not only venture out into the sunlight, he could turn it into any number of machines, most notably, one that could fly—the perfect way to quickly transport the children across a vast distance.

With the children and Nightlight trapped within his lead cloak, Pitch had transformed the djinni into just such a machine.

He cared nothing for beauty, but he appreciated the elaborate design of the flying sleigh machine that swelled out from the djinni's shoulders, back, and arms—every floorboard, deck, and bolt was a mechanical marvel. A surge of envy roiled through him, for it was clearly a combination of ancient magic and human invention that had created this masterpiece. The Nightmare King had never imagined anything that even approached North's genius. But he would. Oh, once he had all the books in the wizard's library, he would.

He narrowed his eyes and issued a curt command to the djinni. "Take me to the core!"

Propellers began to spin, and within seconds, the sleigh was piloting across the sky, crossing continents, then oceans, finally landing upon one of the most desolate places on Earth: a volcano at the very top of the Andes Mountains.

Inside the cloak, the children of Santoff Claussen whispered to one another about where they might be and whether or not Ombric and North had already started their rescue mission.

William the Absolute Youngest fumed in the darkness. "I wish I had a sword," he muttered.

"I do too!" said his oldest brother. "If I had North's new sword, why, I'd—"

"Silence!" roared Pitch. The volcano was a shortcut to his new lair. As they entered the open fissure of the volcano, the flying machine's propellers folded tight. They were speeding down faster and faster, straight for the center of the Earth.

The children, trapped in the inky darkness of Pitch's cloak, could see almost nothing, though their ears began to pop. Their only light was Nightlight's considerably diminished glow.

Tall William and Petter, aided by Fog, tried to push their way out of the cloak prison—to no avail. The black cloth wasn't woven, but made of a metal mesh that was flexible but impenetrable, no matter how hard the boys pushed and clawed at it. Sascha did her best to comfort William the Absolute Youngest and some of the other children, but she was most concerned about Nightlight. He lay slumped against the cloak, his eyes closed. His light grew more and more faint—it started to flicker.

William the Absolute Youngest cried out, "Is he dying?" Tears slipped down the children's cheeks. They held their breaths, watching and hoping that the youngest William was wrong.

Sascha grasped Nightlight's hand. It felt strange in hers, like it was made of air and light and crystals, but in a moment he began to glow—faintly—again, and she breathed a sigh of relief.

To her surprise, Nightlight reached out, collected her tears in his hand, and then did the same with those of the other children. He closed his fist tight around them, before pulling his fist to his chest. The children could see where the bookworm was hiding under Nightlight's jacket. "I hope Mr. Qwerty is all right," said Sascha.

"Remember," whispered Petter, "we mustn't tell Pitch about Mr. Qwerty." Just as they were all nodding in agreement, they slammed down on a rocky surface. The children tumbled onto a hard floor, scraping their knees and elbows. Then Pitch flung open his coat, sending them spinning and rolling in all directions. Sascha banged into a wall. Petter rolled away from Pitch's raised foot only seconds before he brought it down, hard. Tall William did his best to gather the youngest children in a tight group.

They were in a giant room with walls of grayish melted-looking metal. The air reeked of sulfur— shallow pools of milky lava flowed around one end of the room. The children could feel Fearlings weaving in and out of their legs like shadowy black cats. Fog flinched and batted furiously at one that seemed to be whispering in his ear. Sascha pressed her lips together and swallowed a scream as another slithered around her face and head.

Nightlight had helped them see inside the cloak, but here the walls seemed to absorb his dim glow, leaving them in a darkness so thick that they began to wonder if Pitch had swallowed up all the light in the world.

Then there was a sound like fingers snapping, and blue flames appeared from the lava pools, casting everything in an eerie glow. The Fearlings pulled back from the light, but couldn't resist continuing to reach for the children, their long, tentacle-like fingers creeping within inches of their faces.

The older boys drew the younger children behind them, and they all instinctively formed a protective circle around Nightlight.

Pitch smirked at their efforts. He commanded the djinni suit to transform itself back into a mechanical man. Then an inky vapor rose out of the djinni's ear, oozing outward and sharpening into the shape Pitch most preferred for himself. He kicked the mechanical suit aside and loomed over his hostages.

Sascha felt the hands of the smaller children reaching for hers, pulling at her sleeves. She forced herself to stay calm. Ombric, North, and Katherine would move Heaven and Earth to come to their rescue; she knew that as surely as she knew that the sky was blue, the grass was green, and fireflies cheated at games of tag. Still, she couldn't keep herself from averting her eyes as Pitch's gaze lingered on each of them. When he reached Tall William, however, the boy stared back.

"You said you had no plans to hurt us," Tall William said as Pitch loomed over him.

"I remember what I said, boy," Pitch answered. "If your precious wizard hands over his library, perhaps I'll keep my promise. Or perhaps not." Then he pointed his long skeleton arms toward Nightlight.

"But you," he added with a malevolent smile aimed directly at the spectral boy, "you are another story."

Nightlight stared back at Pitch with a weak but mischievous grin. The children's strength was feeding his own, and his light was steadily brightening.

He thought of Katherine, of how much he wanted to see her again, and became stronger still. He had spent thousands of years trapped inside this monster. He could survive whatever it wanted to do to him now.

Enraged by Nightlight's smirk, Pitch raised his hand as if to crush him. Sascha shrieked, but Nightlight's grin only grew wider.

"I'll turn you into my Fearling prince," Pitch threatened. "And your friend, Katherine—when she arrives—will be my princess."

Nightlight knew exactly what Pitch was doing: trying to frighten him by threatening Katherine. He deliberately smiled wider.

Pitch reached out his long, gnarly hand and, with agonizing slowness, let his fingers hover just an inch from Nightlight's head. "Now *you* will be *mine*. You kept me imprisoned for centuries. Day after day, year after year, I dreamed of revenge. . . ." He lowered his hand, but the instant he gripped Nightlight, there was a brilliant explosion of light, sending Pitch staggering backward.

He grasped his hand in pain, and for a moment his palm and fingers seemed to glow, then became flesh-colored. The look on Pitch's face was an unsettling mix of fury and something else. Something the children had never expected to see. Something that looked like . . . sorrow.

Pitch screamed. He covered his injured hand with his cloak, pulled out his sword with his other, then pointed toward a small, cramped cell that hung suspended from the ceiling. A swarm of Fearlings picked up Nightlight and threw him inside the small lead cage. "Please be my guest," Pitch said, his voice suddenly taking on a cheerful tone, "in this solid lead prison, created especially for *you*."

Pitch slammed the door with the tip of his sword. The sword's point then transformed and sharpened into the shape of a key. He locked the door, and the key transformed back into his sword.

"The only way to open that door now will be to kill me," he said with a gleeful smile. "And who amongst you is up to that?!"

Then he laughed in a way that left the children feeling helpless.

CHAPTER EIGHTEEN

A Surprising Twist with a Chocolate Center

THE RABBIT AND NORTH eyed each other, sizing one another up.

North had been dubious about this fabled Rabbit Man since Ombric had first described him. North liked to think that he and Ombric were the world's greatest hero and wizard. The idea of this *rabbit* as their equal—perhaps their superior—did not sit well with the prideful Nicholas St. North. But he would give the Pooka a chance.

"You've been expecting us?" North asked wryly.

"Yes and no. I have and I haven't. Maybe. Maybe

not. I did, however, have an inkling," the rabbit answered. He opened one of his egg-shaped pockets and withdrew some egg-shaped candies. Their outer shells were pebbled with an astonishing variety of delicately iced decorations. "Please, have a chocolate. I make the best in the universe," the rabbit said.

That was the sweet scent Katherine had noticed earlier—chocolate—but this was so alluring that she could barely think of anything else. This wasn't just a whiff of some common candy; it was a hypnotizing mist of taste possibility.

"This one has a caramel center made with the milk of an intergalactic bovine creature that on occasion jumps over the Moon," the Pooka told her, waving it under her nose. "And this one—marshmallow made from the whipped eggs of Asian peacocks!" Bunnymund's eyes glistened. His nose twitched and he leaned forward, holding out a pair of chocolates.

Katherine wavered—she was so hungry. In all their dashing about, she and North hadn't remembered to pack anything to eat. So she reached for one of the chocolates.

Before North could object, the Pooka turned to him. "You, sir, would likely enjoy something darker . . . wilder." He pulled forth a candy of impressive size. "This egg is made with cacao leaves that grow in the dark center of the great caves of Calcutta; it contains a pinch of mint from the ice caps of Mars. It also has three molecules of Hawaiian lava sprouts for a little extra kick."

Never had North smelled something so tantalizing. It was almost as tempting as the jewels the Spirit of the Forest had used to lure his band of outlaws in the enchanted forest. She had turned his men into stone elves, so he couldn't help but be a little suspicious of this offering. Besides, the Pooka's egg warriors were still pointing their bows at them.

"You have a piece first," North countered.

"I should," the rabbit agreed. Then he sighed. "But I shouldn't. Couldn't. Shan't. Won't. It's a long story, full of woe."

That made not a lick of sense to North. But he could not resist the chocolate egg—he was even hungrier than Katherine was. "All right, but call off your warriors," he demanded.

"Yes, of course." Bunnymund waved a paw, and the eggs lowered their weapons and stepped away in perfect unison. *Impressive,* North noted, *and deeply peculiar.* He decided that the Pooka was probably harmless enough, but still, one could never be entirely sure.

The air was rich with an overwhelming scent of chocolate, and Katherine could resist its spell no longer. She had been waiting politely for North to take a chocolate before eating her own, but now she popped the caramel egg into her mouth. A look of bliss crossed her face. Her eyes closed.

Both North and Bunnymund watched her carefully—North out of concern, and Bunnymund with an eagerness to hear her reaction. Katherine began to sway slowly back and forth as if in a dream. She was bewitched by the chocolatey goodness.

The Pooka could wait no longer. "You liked it?" he asked, a single twitching whisker betraying his intense interest.

Katherine smiled, her mouth still flooded with the flavor even after she'd swallowed the candy. "The best chocolate I ever had or thought I would ever have!" she answered dreamily.

"Perfect!" said the rabbit, the rest of his whiskers

now twitching along with his nose.

Then he slammed his staff against the ground, and the Earth opened up beneath them. Katherine and North tumbled forward, spinning down a hole that seemed to be digging itself as they fell. Clumps of rock and dirt whirled past them.

When they stopped, the hole above them closed, and they saw that their chamber led to another egg-shaped chamber, and another and another. There was an endless row of them, stretching as far as they could see. Hundreds of living eggs of various sizes, designs, and uniforms strode about on their toothpick-thin legs, engaged in a wide array of duties. Mixing chocolate. Making candy eggs. Decorating eggs. Painting eggs. Polishing eggs. Packaging eggs. It was all very, very egg-centric.

Katherine gazed about in wonder, then spied

A warrior chocolatier egg

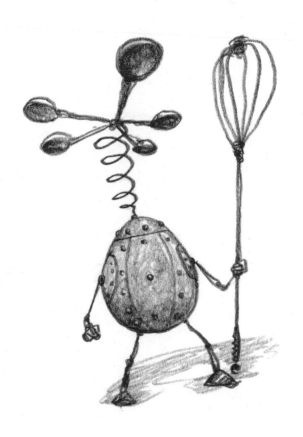

something familiar in a chamber up ahead. It was their ship! Bunnymund had somehow brought it underground too. She sighed with relief: Now she wouldn't have to worry about Kailash being left behind. Still, she wanted Kailash to stay put until she was completely sure this strange underground world was safe.

"Come," Bunnymund invited them, gesturing grandly. "I have much to show you." They passed a vast display of every conceivable type of egg. "I have eggs from every species that ever laid them," Bunnymund said expansively. "Dodo birds, pterodactyls, dinosaurs, the Egg Men of Quacklandia . . ."

On one wall North and Katherine saw a picture of a familiar green and blue planet, only it was egg-shaped, not round. "Is that supposed to be Earth?" Katherine asked.

Bunnymund traced the image reverently. "Yes, many zillions of years ago," he answered. "At that time it was egg-shaped. Unfortunately, ovals have an unstable orbit. If left unchecked, the planet would have swirled closer and closer to the sun and eventually been cooked like a hard-boiled egg."

Katherine stared again at the picture. "But . . . how did it become round?"

"Oh, I fixed it—a nip here, a tuck there," the Pooka said matter-of-factly. "It's rather sad, really. Ovals are such an interesting shape. And circles? Well, so ordinary, common, *dull*." Then he sighed deeply as if saving the planet had been a particularly distressing household chore. "I used the excess dirt to make a few more continents. Australia is my best work, I think," he said. "I'm quite good at digging."

Katherine blinked. "You made *Australia*?"

"Right after I finished the Himalayas," he replied. His whiskers gave a twitch. "But enough geography; I have many, many more eggs to show you."

He spun on a back paw and leaned in toward Katherine. "The egg is the most perfect shape in the universe, don't you agree?"

"We do," Katherine said, nodding enthusiastically, sensing that this would please the rabbit and that pleasing him would make things go faster. "But, well, we're in a hurry. Our friends are in trouble, and our teacher, Ombric Shalazar, believes you can help us." Katherine looked hopefully at him.

"The wizard from Atlantis," Bunnymund said, his ears now twitching. "I had high hopes for that city, but then it vanished." He shook his head. "I did what I could, but . . . humans."

Katherine wasn't sure how to respond to this, but

she had to keep him on subject. She tried to make her face express chagrin at being a mere human, then she pressed on. "Can you help us get to the Earth's core from here?"

Impatience was bubbling up inside North. The light on his sword was blinking more and more frequently, which could only mean that they must be very close to the relic. "Blast it, Man Rabbit! We need your help! We need the Moon relic and we need to get going. Will you help us or not?" he demanded.

Bunnymund sniffed. "I am neither a rabbit nor a man. I am a Pooka. The name is Bunnymund. E. Aster Bunnymund, to be precise."

He leaned forward and asked Katherine, "What other chocolates would you care to try, human girl?"

North had never liked being dismissed, and his temper was about to turn blistering, so Katherine jumped in before he could say anything more, trying to remain polite. "It's not easy to choose," she said, trying to sound confounded.

The Pooka stared at her. She had to do something to make him like them. So she began to lick the last dustings of chocolate from her fingers.

Bunnymund watched her closely. "You do love my chocolate," he said. But then he looked rather glum. "If only chocolate didn't . . . ," and he stopped.

"Didn't what?" Katherine encouraged.

Bunnymund closed his eyes and breathed in. "Alas," he sighed, "chocolate is bad for Pookas."

Well, this is interesting, North thought. *The Pooka surrounds himself with what tempts him the most.* He gave Bunnymund an appraising stare. "Bad how?" he asked.

Bunnymund shot him a look. "It makes me more like you. Illogical. Racing about. Always trying to save the day." He shook his head, as if disgusted with himself.

North began to object to the rabbit's tone, but Bunnymund had turned his back to them and was now throwing open the door of a cabinet filled top to bottom with shelves of chocolate eggs. The display was dazzling.

Katherine stopped him. "You've been very generous," she said. "But we'd be most grateful if you would let us borrow the relic—and help us get to the Earth's core. Please."

"Oh, no, no, no," the Pooka said, pulling out a tray of confections. "My expertise is in chocolate. I don't get involved in human affairs. Not anymore."

"Untrue!" said North. "You stopped Ombric from changing history when *he* went back in time. Twice!"

"Indeed. But tampering with the past is not allowed for any living creature—Man, Beast, Plant, or Egg. I've been watching that Ombric of yours since he was a boy. He doesn't believe in rules very much."

"Yes," agreed North. "Especially stupid ones."

The rabbit didn't seem to like North's manner.

Katherine shrewdly changed the subject. "You know what Pitch did to the Golden Age. Don't you want to stop him from doing any more damage?"

Bunnymund shrugged. "Humans come. Humans go. They leave many relics. I've been on the planet much longer than humans have, and I will be here long after there are no more."

"Balderdash!" said North. "So you won't help us?"

"My dear fellow, I didn't say I wouldn't help you," Bunnymund replied. "I am just not *interested* in helping you."

North and Katherine did not know how to respond.

CHAPTER NINETEEN

Nightlight Is Dimmed

DEEPER BELOW GROUND THAN any human had ever ventured, the children of Santoff Clausen hung in metal cages in the center of the Earth. The cages, which hovered a few feet above the floor, were freshly made just for them. The strange swirling shapes of hastily poured molten lead surrounding them was full of airholes and gaps so the children, at least, could see out. There was much activity around them. Countless Fearlings were building and shaping innumerable lead weapons, armor plates, and shields. The children could hear Pitch's frenzied shouting of orders and they looked repeatedly toward Nightlight's prison for reassurance. Just knowing he was nearby helped, which was the only comfort they had.

Unlike their cages, Nightlight's prison was made of solid lead. There wasn't a window, there wasn't a crack, there wasn't a pinhole. And the door was sealed so tight, no light could make its way inside.

Nightlight lay on the floor of the cage. He did not move. His eyes were closed. His light grew dimmer with every passing minute. The lead seemed to be leaching all his brightness from him. But Nightlight was not alone.

Something stirred under his jacket. And for a moment Nightlight glowed brighter.

CHAPTER TWENTY

In Which We Find Munch Marks of Mystery

BACK IN SANTOFF CLAUSSEN, Ombric was slowly and carefully releasing prisoners of another sort: the residents of the village who were caught in Pitch's enslavement spell. It haunted him to see his beloved village, the focus of his long and brilliant life, frozen in a moment of struggle and terror. He began with Petrov, the bear, and the Spirit of the Forest, for they would need to keep watch in case the Fearlings were planning to attack again.

As they stamped and roared and spun themselves awake, Ombric told them the terrible news of the children's capture. Despair hung over them like a shroud—they had failed to protect the children from Pitch. Ombric urged them not to blame themselves.

"Even I once was caught by Pitch in such a spell," he explained. Urgently, he told them that Pitch was holding the children hostage and that the library was the ransom he demanded. None of them knew where his books had gone, so Ombric moved on to release the owls and the other creatures in Big Root. They seemed the most likely to be able to help him solve the mystery.

To each creature raised from Pitch's spell, Ombric asked the same questions: "What happened to the books in my library? Where are they?"

And each time he got the same answer. No one knew. But from the moonbeam, Ombric *had* learned one important detail: His shelves were already empty when Pitch smashed into the library.

Before she had left, Katherine had carefully gathered the pieces of Nightlight's shattered diamond dagger and placed them in a box. It was in this box where the moonbeam now rested. The poor little fellow seemed comforted to be with the diamond shards that had become his home, and Ombric found himself wondering if the dagger could ever be repaired. It was the physical manifestation of the Man in the Moon's spirit and of Nightlight's courage, forged during that last great battle of the Golden Age. But now Ombric knew that the dagger could not be used to hurt anyone or anything good. That was why it had shattered when Pitch tried to kill Nightlight with it.

Once all the creatures in Big Root were up and

stretching, Ombric headed outside. He had saved the parents for last. They had likely been unconscious while under Pitch's spell, so he would have to tell them that their children had been taken.

The parents seemed to have just reached Big Root when Pitch had bewitched them, for that's where they lay, most of them on their sides or on their backs, where they had fallen when the Nightmare King turned them into toys. Their china faces expressed dread and alarm, the only exception being Old William's.

Ombric released him first. Old William contorted his lips again and again to get them moving. Then, as soon as he was able to speak, the father of all the Williams told Ombric his story: "I'm no swordsman, but I fought with all my might. We used stardust bombs against him! But they did nothing. His cloak and sword sucked up all the light! He stormed

Big Root, boasting that he was going to be a more powerful wizard than you."

Old William's voice cracked with desperation. "Will I see my Williams again?" he asked.

"Yes," Ombric promised him.

Old William walked with Ombric as he moved from parent to parent, transforming them from tiny, porcelain versions of themselves back into living, breathing human beings. And Ombric told them to be brave, that their children had been taken hostage.

He met the gaze of each and every parent, taking in their worried frowns and wishing he could ease their burdens. "Nicholas St. North and Katherine are on their way to the Earth's core even now," he told them. "I will do my utmost to find the books Pitch covets, and when I do, they'll make the exchange. But I must know where the books are."

But all the parents assured Ombric that the children had been working on lessons in his library up until the moment Pitch's Fearlings began to seep into the enchanted forest.

"And yet all the books disappeared *before* Pitch could get to them," Ombric mused, stroking his beard.

The Spirit of the Forest hovered above him. "He took pleasure in what he had done to us," she told him. "He swaggered about, enjoying his handiwork." She began to weep tears of angry frustration. They hardened to emeralds and pearls that spilled uselessly to the ground, reminding her once again that her treasures were not what Pitch was after.

Ombric grew increasingly puzzled, and as soon as every living being in Santoff Claussen had been restored, he returned to his shattered library to investigate more diligently. The owls could remember nearly nothing. They'd seen a flash of light just as Nightlight rushed in. He made what looked like a protective shield around the children with it. Then Pitch's spell began to take hold of the owls, and everything had gone dark. Ombric saw that bit of information as a clue. He plucked up one of the tiny scraps of paper that littered the floor, turning it over and over. He held it up to the light and noticed funny little markings on one edge. He picked up another scrap, then another. They all had the same choppy shapes along one edge.

Ombric sat back in his chair, closed his eyes, and tried to remember where he had seen similar markings. Suddenly, it hit him.

"Teeth marks!" he exclaimed. "Those are teeth marks!"

CHAPTER TWENTY-ONE

The Egg-cellent Exchange

Bunnymund's "just not interested" still hung in the air.

The Pooka's nose twitched, and with a sharp twist of his staff, he disappeared.

Katherine and North were alone.

"I think you made him mad," said Katherine.

"Who needs his help?" North declared. "Let's find that relic ourselves. Perhaps it can get us out of here and to the Earth's core." He let his sword lead them. Its blade pulled them through one egg-shaped chamber after another.

The first few chambers were similar to the one they had already been in—equipped for candy making. One smelled curiously of cinnamon and another of a sweetness that was so powerful and tempting, they had to fight the urge to stop and inhale its trancelike perfection forever.

But the next chamber they found themselves in was a curious kind of egg museum. There were shelves upon shelves of intricately crafted, jewel-encrusted eggs.

North whistled. "I know a Russian tsar who would pay a fortune for some of these," he said appraisingly as the sword pulled him on to yet another chamber.

The next room, too, was a kind of museum, but the eggs here were natural. A bumpy yellow and orange shell labeled SEA MONSTER sat beside the green speckled egg of a MESOPOTAMIAN DRAGON.

Rows and rows of eggshells lined the walls, ranging from the giant egg of a mega-octopus (pure white and bigger than North's head) to the miniature ones of a hummingbird (smaller than Katherine's thumbnail). There were chicken eggs and goose eggs, duck eggs and swan eggs, and even the tiny illuminated yellow eggs of a glowworm, barely the size of pinpricks. There were so many sizes and colors and patterns and speckles that these eggs seemed to Katherine to be even more beautiful than the eggs carved of gold and jewels. Then North let out a long, slow whistle.

Katherine ran to the next room.

Inside was just a single egg. It sat on a podium of gleaming silver. The egg looked as if it were made of the same mysterious metal as North's sword and was covered in gorgeously wrought carvings of suns and moons and stars. At its center was a crescent Moon that glowed with the same intensity as the orb on the magic sword. In fact, the egg and the sword seemed to be reaching for each other.

"That's it!" North cried out triumphantly. "That's the relic!"

He raced forward, reaching out to snatch up the egg. But before he could get his hand on it, he found himself being hurtled across the room. He landed against the wall, his head pounding.

When he could focus again, Bunnymund was standing over him. "Naughty. Naughty," he said.

North jumped to his feet, rubbing the back of his head. "Did you do that?" he shouted.

Bunnymund again went so still that he didn't appear to be breathing. Then his nose twitched.

Katherine sensed a fight coming on. So, it seemed, did the Warrior Eggs. A mass of them trotted into the chamber on their tiny legs, bows again at the ready. Katherine ran over to stand between North and the Pooka.

"That egg does not belong to you," the rabbit told North firmly.

North clenched his teeth to keep from yelling. "Don't get your whiskers in a twist, Man Bunny," he said. "I doubt you even know the power and significance of that precious egg of yours! That it was fashioned by *people*, not by rabbits or Pookas, but humans from an age more grand than you can imagine. And that it was intended for purposes of good and honor and bravery, not to be used as some useless bauble that satisfies the puny whims of your precious collection!"

It was clear that North's argument had a powerful effect on Bunnymund. The rabbit stepped closer.

He then stood ramrod straight while his nose and whiskers twitched and stilled. Twitched and stilled. The twitches were soon as fast and blurred as the wings of a hummingbird in flight. Then the Pooka spoke very calmly and firmly.

"I know the egg's powers and its origins quite well, Mr. North. I helped, in fact, to make it." He paused for a moment, letting North absorb that information. He drew himself taller, adding, "Inside its curved shell is the purest light in all creation. Light from the exact beginning of time. It is the light that all Pookas were sworn to wield and protect. But men, *people*, cannot be trusted with it. We tried once, during the Golden Age."

"Fine! Then *you* must help us stop Pitch," North pressed. "*He* killed the Golden Age! He is a creature! A monster—"

"But," Bunnymund interrupted, "he was first a man."

North was not ready with a fast retort, but the Pooka raised his hand as if he were and continued: "Pookas were the gatherers of this light. We brought it to worlds that we felt were ready for its power. We thought that the people of the Golden Age showed the most promise of all, and they used it well. But then Pitch came. He destroyed everything. He is why I am the last of my kind. I came here with the hope of a new Golden Age." He fixed North with a stare. "That is why Tsar Lunar, the Man in the Moon's father, sent this 'relic,' as you call it, to me.

"And since it has been in my possession, I've tried over and over to help the world of humans. I've invented most of your trees, flowers, grass. Spring. Jokes. Summer vacations. Recess. Chocolate. But none of it seems to have changed anything. Humans still behave badly and never seem to cherish the light." A look that could only be described as forlorn crossed the Pooka's face, and his voice grew solemn. "Man cannot be trusted."

"All that you invented—all of it—will be lost if Pitch has his way," argued North. "He'll drain *all* the light out of the world. Can you let that happen?"

Bunnymund seemed to think about that for a moment.

"Pitch and his Fearlings don't even like chocolate or *eggs!*" Katherine added. She wasn't sure if that was true, but it sounded good.

Bunnymund was deeply disturbed by that remark. He puzzled. And puzzled. The egg warriors seemed unsure. They lowered their weapons a few inches. Finally, the rabbit spoke.

"The fiends! Not like chocolate? Not like"—he gasped—"eggs? Now, won't you please stop talking—you humans use so many, many words. And so few of them are about eggs. It's exhausting."

Bunnymund eased the relic from its shimmering stand and held it aloft. "I will return in approximately one hour and seven minutes, human time—with your friends."

"I'm ready," North said. "Let's go."

"Oh, no, no, no," Bunnymund said. "I work alone."

CHAPTER TWENTY-TWO

One Mystery Begets Another

"Teeth marks!" Ombric said again. "But *whose* teeth marks?" His beard twirled as he pondered.

His exclamation echoed throughout the village. The creatures of the forest, bristling with pent-up energy after having been trapped as toys for so long, joined forces to help Ombric search for clues. Dragonflies and moths flew through every inch of the forest. Spiders and ants crawled into every hidden nook in Big Root. Birds and squirrels checked the treetops.

The parents, too, joined the search, combing

through every home and every yard, upending mattresses and vegetable gardens.

Ombric examined the gnawed pieces of paper with his microscope. "Who would eat my books? Nightlight had some hand in it, I'm sure, but what . . . ," he wondered. He pressed his fingers against his temples, not wanting to admit it, but his last journey through time had taken a great toll on him. The long, slow process of releasing the entire village from Pitch's spell had added to his weariness. For the first time in his very long life, Ombric felt not old but ancient. But he couldn't wallow in this unfamiliar feeling—the children needed him, old or not. So he shook away his fatigue and examined the paper scraps again.

Mr. Qwerty would never allow—

Ombric stopped in midsentence. His eyebrows,

beard, mustache, hair, shoes, and even eyelashes began to twirl.

"MR. QWERTY!" Ombric shouted, leaping up. "MR. QWERTY!! MR. QWEEEEERTY!!!" He hadn't seen the glowworm since he returned to the village! And now he knew the reason. "Mr. Qwerty has eaten my books! To keep them out of Pitch's hands!"

First things first. He remembered what the owls had said: They saw a flash of light before everything had gone dark. Ombric opened the box where the moonbeam rested and asked, "Was Nightlight holding anything when Pitch took him away?"

The moonbeam, sensing Ombric's excitement, grew stronger himself and glowed: *Yes.*

"Was it white? Rather oblong? About the size of my hand?"

The moonbeam pulsed twice.

"That's it!" Ombric said, sitting back down with a knowing nod. "Mr. Qwerty ate the books! Then he wrapped himself in a cocoon! Nightlight's flash of light protected the children and gave Mr. Qwerty time to eat the books. The little fellow was always hungry for knowledge, but this is *epic!*" Ombric was almost laughing now. "Nightlight took Mr. Qwerty! He has him still. The library is in Mr. Qwerty's stomach."

The old wizard stroked his still-twirling beard. "Right under Pitch's nose. . . ."

CHAPTER TWENTY-THREE

The Honk of Destiny

WE WILL NEVER KNOW what furious argument might have followed Bunnymund's insistence that he go to the Earth's core without North and Katherine, for in the incredibly tense seconds after the Pooka had made his declaration, Kailash came waddling into the chamber and honked loudly.

They all three turned and looked at the goose— North with slight irritation, Katherine with concern, and Bunnymund with complete and total awe.

"Is this one of the Great Snow Geese of the Himalayas?" Bunnymund asked, his nose not twitching but sort of rotating slowly in amazement.

"Yes. Her name is Kailash," Katherine told him hesitantly, a little rattled by the rabbit's shift in interest. "She thinks I'm her mother. I was there when she hatched."

The Pooka inhaled deeply. "Tell me everything," he insisted. "Was the egg very beautiful?"

North fought his every impulse not to shake some sense into this strange, long-eared creature. Time was tumbling by, and the rabbit wanted to talk about eggs! But North's calmer self sensed an opportunity.

"Tell him about the blasted egg," he said, motioning to Katherine to hurry.

Katherine put an arm around Kailash's slender neck. "Well, her egg was large and silvery, with swirls of pebble-size bumps that glistened like diamonds and opals," she said.

"As I've always imagined it! Come," Bunnymund said, pointing to his egg museum. One of the shelves had an empty space labeled HIMALAYAN GREAT SNOW GOOSE. "It's the one egg I don't have. My collection is not complete." He stared at Katherine. "It's silvery, you say?"

"Silvery and blue," Katherine elaborated.

The Pooka could scarcely contain himself.

"Kailash would be grateful to anyone who did as we asked," Katherine said.

The Pooka was almost quivering. After a long moment his former reserve seemed to return. His nose twitched. Then he spoke: "My army is already assembled. I am at the ready. As I hope you are. Any friends of the Great Snow Geese are friends of mine. Come this way. We'll take tunnel number seventeen twenty-eight." He paused dramatically, then added with a flourish, "Straight to the Earth's core!"

"Finally," North grumbled, placing his hand on the hilt of the magic sword. The weapon began to glow. Bunnymund's egg relic did the same.

CHAPTER TWENTY-FOUR

In Which There Is a Fearful Discovery and a Whisper of Hope

O THE CHILDREN'S GREAT relief, Pitch and his Fearlings had disappeared into another chamber.

The chamber where they were kept was as wide and as tall as Big Root. But it was nothing like Big Root. This was a dark and fretful place. If Big Root was a treasure chest of wonders, Pitch's lair at the Earth's core was like the fabled box of Pandora: filled with doom and darkness. The children had managed to ever so quietly wiggle through the openings in their cages and climb down. Half a dozen tunnels led out from the chamber, but Tall William and Petter had explored and reported that every one was being guarded by Fearlings. Not that it mattered. The children wouldn't try to escape without Nightlight.

Fog, Petter, and Sascha stood watch while Tall William ran his hands over the door of Nightlight's cage, seeking a knob, a keyhole, anything that would help them free their friend. But there was nothing, not even a crack. Whatever dark magic Pitch had used when he removed his sword from the lock had left the door smoother than fresh ice on the skating pond in Santoff Claussen.

Tall William knocked hard to let Nightlight know that he was there, then placed his ear against the cage.

"Did he hear you?" Sascha asked, putting her own ear against the metal. "Did he knock back?"

Tall William shook his head. "I don't think so,

but it's hard to hear anything with all that banging going on."

That banging was the incessant clamor—clanking, hammering, striking—coming from the next chamber. Every now and again it was peppered by the Nightmare King's booming laugh.

"What do you think Pitch is up to?" Petter whispered.

"Let's find out," Tall William whispered back.

They crept stealthily to the entrance of the next chamber and peered around the wall, just out of sight of the Fearling guards.

What they saw made their eyes go wide. Hundreds of Fearlings were working furiously under Pitch's direction. Some were chipping away at the lead walls, making the room larger, dropping the lead chips into a bucket. Other Fearlings melted buckets of lead over an eerie blue lava. When the lead melted into a sticky liquid, they poured the mixture into molds.

Tall William watched uneasily—something was different about these Fearlings. They seemed more solid, less shadowy, than the others. One of them tested the lead in a mold with a thin rod. It was solid now, and the Fearling popped what looked like a heavy vest out of the mold and then handed it to the creature next to him. They passed it from one to the next, down the line, until it reached a Fearling that looked normal. Or at least what Tall William and the others had come to think of as normal. The creature slipped the object over his shadowy body. Then he, too, took on the more solid look of the others and skulked into the light.

"They're making armor," Tall William breathed out.

Petter stared hard. "It covers them completely."

"Now they'll be able to go out in the sunlight!" whispered Tall William, struggling to keep the dread out of his voice.

Then they saw rows of swords and spears being fashioned from the same thick liquid.

"Like Pitch's sword!" Petter hissed.

They crept back to the others and reported what they had seen.

The smaller children just stared after hearing this alarming news. The smallest William hid his head under Fog's arm.

Sascha drew a deep breath to keep her voice steady, then said, "I wish Ombric and the others would hurry."

Tall William tried hard not to seem scared, but he was. "The Fearlings will be too strong for them now with that armor and those weapons," he said quietly.

Petter grew very serious. "And if they bring Ombric's library, Pitch will know all the magic there is!" he said. "He'll be unstoppable.

"But we mustn't be afraid," he added, trying to convince himself as well as the others. "It only makes Pitch stronger."

The children knew he was right. But it was getting very hard to stay brave.

If they'd only been able to hear the conversation that was taking place inside Nightlight's tiny, cramped cage. Nightlight was listening to the muffled voice of Mr. Qwerty. The cocoon shifted and wiggled under his jacket. "Change is coming," said the valiant little worm. "And it cannot be stopped."

And Nightlight brightened.

CHAPTER TWENTY-FIVE

ℑhe 𝔈gg 𝔄rmada

I F THERE ARE SEVEN Wonders of the Known World, Bunnymund's tunnel to the Earth's core would be the first of the *unknown* world. It was shaped like an egg standing on end and seemed to go on forever. North was intrigued by how quietly the Pooka's train was traveling. Despite their remarkable speed, the train barely made a sound, just a quiet sort of clucking noise. He'd have to ask the Pooka how he managed that . . . even the mechanical djinni had emitted squeaks and hums.

And though Katherine was increasingly worried

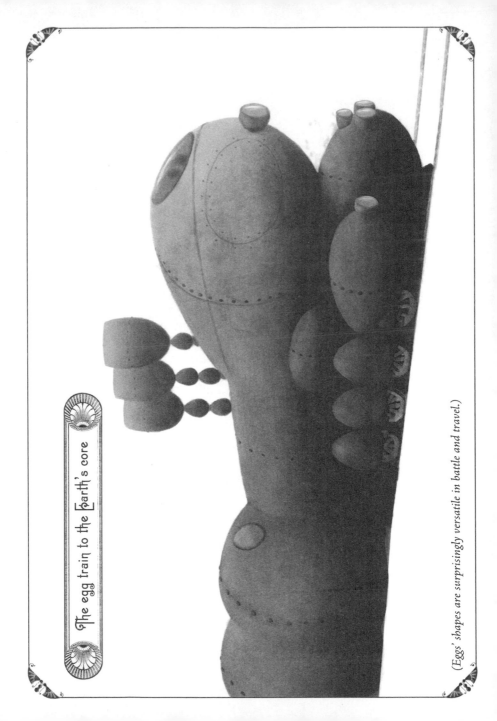

The egg train to the Earth's core

(Eggs' shapes are surprisingly versatile in battle and travel.)

about Nightlight and her friends, she couldn't help noticing how enticingly strange everything about Bunnymund's conveyance was. The railroad cars that were whisking them deeper and deeper underground were of course egg-shaped, as was virtually every knob, hinge, door, window, light fixture, and mechanical component. It was even more opulent than the Lamas' flying tower.

Plus, the cars immediately behind her held an imposing army of well-armored Warrior Eggs wielding an impressive array of weaponry. The smallest eggs were the size of a common chicken's egg, while platoons of other eggs were nearly as big as a good-sized suitcase, and a surprising number of eggs were huge—more than ten feet tall. Katherine was very interested about where *those* eggs could have come from!

North, on the other hand, was having a difficult time taking these Warrior Eggs seriously. *They're eggs!* he thought to himself. *EGGS!* But he tried not to betray his doubts and instead asked his host in a tone that at least hinted at politeness, "Very pretty eggs, Bunnymund, but can they fight?"

The Pooka regarded him evenly, his nose not even twitching. "The Greeks thought so at Troy," he replied, sounding a bit bored. "Though why they built that clumsy horse instead of an egg, as I suggested, I'll never understand."

Katherine, sensing another potential argument brewing, thought it best to interrupt. "Are we getting close?" she asked.

"At our current rate of speed, we'll be there in exactly thirty-seven clucks," Bunnymund replied.

Clucks? North and Katherine both wondered,

then decided not to ask any more questions for a while. Bunnymund's answers always left them feeling, well, they just weren't sure. Bewildered? Uncertain? Odd? Doomed?

Meanwhile, Bunnymund regarded the two humans. He found himself concerned for them. *But why?* Here was this headstrong young man, so determined to be daring. And the little girl, worrying about her friends. Even that lovely goose was all a-twitter about the danger the girl faced. So much disorder and upheaval!

Still, he had to admit that there was a certain satisfaction in working with others, even humans. Never would he acknowledge that out loud, of course, but the Pooka had been alone for so many, many years. Having these other creatures about presented a change of pace. The girl did have excellent taste in chocolates. And there was something to be said for adventure. And what was this if not an adventure?

Bunnymund's musings were interrupted by an insistent clanging sound—far off at the moment, but growing louder and closer as his train barreled forward.

"We're very nearly there," he told the others.

Katherine could tell, for she could smell the dank, sulfury odor of Fearlings. She held her dagger tighter.

At the same time North's sword and Bunnymund's staff both began to glow. Danger was apparently just ahead.

An egg-straordinary way to travel.

CHAPTER TWENTY-SIX

The Low-Rotten Core

Bunnymund ordered the train to stop, and it did so as smoothly as a duck landing on a pond. He, North, and Katherine made their way to the engine car at the front to better see what was ahead. Engineer eggs were still stoking the egg-shaped boiler of the idling engine with egg-shaped clumps of coal.

"They occur naturally," explained Bunnymund before Katherine could even ask the question. "Egg-shaped coal is where diamonds come from."

Katherine liked knowing that, but North found the information distracting.

"Eggs!" he groused. "You talk too much about eggs!"

Bunnymund was offended.

"I do *not.*"

"You do too."

"I DO NOT!"

"Yes. You. Do."

"Do not!"

"Do too!"

Katherine sighed. Here they were, the oldest and wisest creature on Earth and the greatest warrior-wizard of the age, yet they were behaving like a pair of brats. She'd been waiting for something like this to happen between them. They'd been aching for a fight since they'd met! Truth be told, she'd expected something more mature from them both. *Grown-ups, wizards, and Pookas! Are they all this muddled?* she wondered.

As the "do not"s and "do too"s continued unabated, Katherine made a decision: She would ignore them both. She turned to Kailash and told her to go to the back of the train and stay quiet. The gosling honked sadly, but Katherine insisted. As Kailash waddled back to the passenger cars, Katherine climbed down from the engine and walked down the tunnel. It was very dim. The walls of the tunnel grew less smooth and crafted. The egg-shaped lanterns that had been affixed to the ceiling for the whole length of the passageway thus far now appeared less and less frequently.

As she continued forward, she could barely make out where the tracks ended. The light of the lantern ahead of her—the last one she could see—was mistier than the others had been. Its shine hit in odd directions. Katherine paused, trying to sort out why that was so.

The ominous clanking they'd heard earlier grew louder and louder; she could feel the reverberations. But she continued forward until she stood under the lantern and its strange glow. The light looked as if it were being blown in the wind.

She followed its fading glow as it twisted farther away, but toward what? She took a few more steps forward, following the light. And with each step, the tunnel grew wider and taller—immense, in fact. And then, to her complete surprise, it stopped. Just stopped. A gray vastness loomed in front of her, a giant wall that blocked her from going any farther. But it didn't stop the light; Katherine could see that the misty stream of lantern light was actually flowing into this wall of dense, dark, metallic-looking rock.

And then she knew. She was at the Earth's core.

She approached the wall cautiously, her dagger at the ready. It occurred to her that her weapon couldn't possibly be of use against *a wall*, but perhaps it could defend against what was on the other side of the wall. So she kept her dagger raised, and she listened intently.

The sounds from within were deep and menacing, like growling thunder from an approaching storm. She heard what she thought was . . . laughing. Laughing? Could that be possible? Then she realized that it was Pitch's laugh. A cold shiver ran through her soul.

Katherine reached into her coat pocket and pulled out the locket that she had gotten from Ombric. She looked at the picture of Pitch's daughter. Again she felt a strange sort of sadness. She had lost her father before she'd ever really known him, and yet she missed him every day. Their time together had been so brief, but the bond lived on. She knew it would never fade or die. She studied the picture of that long-ago little girl and wondered: *Might this locket be a much more powerful weapon against Pitch than any dagger?*

Then a shift in the lantern's light caught her attention. The light was changing—twisting down and splitting into different threads, fanning out like a web that arched behind her. She spun around. Surrounding her stood a dozen or so Fearlings. The tendrils of the lantern light fed directly into their leaded armor.

"NORTH!" Katherine managed to scream before they whisked her away to the awful place behind the wall.

CHAPTER TWENTY-SEVEN

The Power of the Inner Pooka

R EMEMBER," NORTH WAS SAYING, glowering at Bunnymund. "Pitch is *mine*." The Pooka's nose twitched.

Then they heard Katherine's scream.

North didn't wait for Bunnymund to respond. He turned on his heels and ran, his sword leading the way as if it couldn't wait to do battle. A knot of Fearlings plunged down at him. He could tell at a glance that they were more formidable than any Fearlings he'd seen before. They looked denser somehow, and though his sword was glowing far more brightly than usual, its light seemed to be sucked into the Fearlings themselves. North was startled. But the hilt of the sword wrapped itself tightly around his hand, and this gave him courage—he literally felt himself becoming stronger, faster. He slashed at the marauders as they descended upon him.

He had expected them to vanish with one quick touch, but they did not. Instead, he heard the clank of metal against metal as he struck at the Fearlings and realized that they were armored, like knights of old, but deformed, tangled, and terrible.

And armed.

How could that be? North managed to think as he lashed out again and again, barely able to stop the Fearlings' heavy swords from carving him up as they swooped down at him like giant murderous bats. They swerved in midair to attack again. North willed himself to be stronger and faster still, and as he did, the sword responded.

When the Fearlings dove at him again, he sliced them down with swift and brutal precision. Their armor hacked open, the Fearlings vanished into nothingness. The empty armor fell to the tunnel floor like hunks from a broken coffin.

North gripped his sword and stood ready for the next onslaught, but none came. In the tense quiet he had time to think one terrible thought: *What has happened to Katherine?*

The sword seemed to respond for, from its hilt, a small oval mirror emerged. At first North saw only his own face and Bunnymund and his army racing from the train behind him. Then the mirror showed another image—blurry at first, then sharper. It was Katherine, surrounded by Fearlings. Then it shifted to the face of Pitch as he looked down at her. The image faded and the mirror grew dark, reflecting nothing.

North gripped his sword so intensely that he began to shake. *This is my fault,* he thought. He'd dropped his guard. Let himself become distracted by—what? By a candy-making rabbit!

Bunnymund came up just behind North. Pookas have an uncanny ability to sense what others think and feel. He knew that North thought he was a silly creature. Ridiculous, even. But that didn't bother him.

He could also sense North's anger and determination, his need to help his young friend. The rabbit had kept his distance from the tumultuous feelings of living things for centuries, but now he knew he must respond as he would have in days of old.

He put his paw on North's shoulder in as friendly a way as a Pooka can. Then he sighed deeply. "Dear fellow," he said to North, "this will be more difficult than I had imagined. Drastic measures are required." He reached into his robe and pulled out three chocolate eggs.

"This is no time for sweets," North snapped in frustration.

"For you, perhaps," said the rabbit, then he popped the three chocolates in his mouth. The Egg Army gasped in almost-perfect unison. None of them had ever seen Bunnymund eat a chocolate. They had only heard rumors of what happened when Pookas ate the substance.

There was a curious rumbling. North turned around to face Bunnymund. The rabbit appeared to be growing before his eyes, becoming huge, then hulking, like a warrior from a mythology not yet written.

Bunnymund raised his egg-tipped staff above his head and let out a yell that shook the tunnel like an earthquake. The army of eggs did likewise. The sound was unlike anything North had ever heard.

It was the first time in a thousand years the world had heard the Pookan war cry.

And even Nicholas St. North was impressed.

CHAPTER TWENTY-EIGHT

The Battle Begins

PITCH HAD ALMOST NO time to relish the capture of Katherine. He knew that if the girl was here, North and Ombric must be near—and the magic library close at hand! But moments after the Fearlings had brought the girl to him, he heard that extraordinary, otherworldly sound.

He alone among all the creatures living had heard that war cry before. It was a sound he'd hoped to never hear again. He remembered it from the time he'd destroyed the Pookan Brotherhood. It was the one battle of the Golden Age he had nearly lost. "They've got a Pooka with them!" he hissed with alarm.

He knew he must act quickly.

"Make ready!" he bellowed to his Fearling Army. "The battle begins!"

The Fearlings gathered with enviable swiftness. Armor ready, weapons raised, they were a force no one would wish to face.

Pitch grabbed Katherine by the collar and dragged her with him. "Come, sprite," he muttered. "I've no time to dally with you just now."

He rushed from chamber to chamber, shouting commands, making sure his dark army was in place and ready, and all the while Katherine dangled at his side like a sack. She watched every movement of the Fearling troops, which was no easy feat, as she was being buffeted about with Pitch's grim grip tight at her neck. But she could see the trap that Pitch was planning. The Fearlings would let North and Bunnymund make their way deep into the hollow of the Earth's core, then surround and overwhelm them.

Her mind raced. As Pitch planned to destroy her friends, she plotted how best to stop him.

The Pookan war cry grew louder and closer. The Egg Army had obviously made it through the wall of lead that surrounded Pitch's lair.

Time was short. Katherine had so few choices, and none played to her favor. But then, as Pitch was hurrying into another chamber, she saw the metal cages holding the children. Her friends!

They'd crawled back up into the cages to avoid detection by Pitch, but Tall William and the others could see her as well. They yelled and stuck their hands through the airholes to wave. She tried to shout back, but Pitch swung her suddenly to his other hand. As he did so, she noticed, for only an instant, that this hand seemed different . . . changed . . . almost human-looking. Then she heard the opening of a metal door, and she was shoved into a small room. The door slammed behind her. She was immersed in a darkness that was total and complete.

And though he did not know it, Pitch had put her in the one place where she most needed to be.

CHAPTER TWENTY-NINE

The Voice

OMBRIC HAD BEEN FURIOUSLY preparing for his trip to the Earth's core. From the moment he'd figured out what had happened to his library and Mr. Qwerty's role in its disappearance, he'd worked nonstop to make a perfect reproduction of it. Every single book, every single history, calculation, chart, map, mixture, blueprint, plan, and spell had been duplicated and set down. The entire village had been busy, binding the texts that Ombric had dictated to the owls (who were brilliantly adept at writing and drawing with both talons at the same time).

It was fortunate that Ombric could call upon his unmatched memory to recite the entire trove of his knowledge.

When the last volume was stitched and bound, Ombric stood back to take in the whole of it. It looked as if his library had never been touched; it looked perfect. But it was all bogus. There were flaws carefully crafted into each bit of information. Because of Ombric's perfect memory, he knew exactly where to make a change here, a switch there. If followed to the letter, not one spell in this entire fabrication would work.

Ombric had no idea what form the real library was in since Mr. Qwerty had bravely devoured it. The wizard was impressed by this brilliant bit of strategy on Mr. Qwerty's and Nightlight's part, but he had to make certain that Pitch did not get the real library—

the phony one would have to be used to trick the villain.

This had been an extremely exhausting task, and he still had to muster the energy to astrally project himself and the immense library all the way to the center of Earth.

He sat in his favorite chair thinking about his store of knowledge. Remembering it had been both satisfying and bittersweet. He felt as though he had relived the entire arc of his life. He remembered learning each and every bit of magic: where he'd been, who he'd been with at the time. He realized that he'd achieved a rich, wild, vivid life. He had lived as he had believed. He had seen and known more wonder than almost any mortal ever had. So he felt a weary satisfaction. He would just need to rest his mind for a while.

Ombric leaned back and tugged at his beard, the

owls watching him worriedly. They had never seen their master so tired, so frail.

Ombric's breathing became quiet and rhythmic, and he drifted into a deep sleep.

He dreamed of when he was just a child in the city of Atlantis. There had been a day in his childhood that had always baffled him—the day of his first magic. And now he seemed to be reliving it. He hadn't been much younger than the youngest William, and had been secretly listening to the lessons of the older children; he had heard knowledge he was not yet supposed to know. He learned the secret of how to make a daydream come true.

The young Ombric stood in an open field and started to recite the spell. It was a difficult enchantment and required great concentration, but he was a boy with a talent for concentration. He focused hard, till his mind was clear of all distraction. He chanted the words slowly and thoughtfully. Ombric had always daydreamed of flying. And after a time he started drifting upward, at first just grazing the top of the tall, green field grass, then higher, and finally up into the sky. He flew in and around clouds, soaring and spiraling like a fantastic sort of bird.

But he had gone too fast and flown too high. His young mind grew tired. He could no longer maintain the spell, and he began to fall. Fear took over his thinking as he plummeted to the ground. He knew he must stop being afraid and focus on the spell, but his pulse was pounding and panic set in.

He began to tumble uncontrollably, spiraling end over end with sickening speed. Everything was a terrifying blur. He fell so fast that he began to black out.

And he was glad. He couldn't stand to feel a terror

this total, and he didn't want to face the instant that was coming—the moment when he would smash to the ground and be no more. As he began to lose consciousness, he felt a strange sort of calm. An acceptance of what would happen. Then he heard a voice whisper to him: "I believe. I believe. I believe." It was a pleasant voice. One he did not recognize, but at the same time, it sounded familiar. And he no longer felt afraid. Then, as all went black, he knew— *knew*—everything would be all right.

And it was. He opened his young eyes some time later. He was in the same green field. He was not hurt. Not a scratch or a bruise was on him. Only his red hair was tousled. Ombric never knew how he had survived or who had spoken the magic words to him. But on that day he had learned the power of fear, that fear was an enemy that must always be conquered.

Then the memory ended, but the dream went on. . . .

Ombric now saw himself in that same field from childhood. He was not a boy anymore but very old. He lay in the soft green grass. It was so cool and comfortable. There was a soothing breeze, and the sky above was alive with white clouds that drifted by like great galleons. *I am so tired. Maybe I will just stay here forever,* he thought. *It is peaceful.*

But now he heard the words again, echoing from far away. But this time the voice was different.

It was a young girl's voice. He struggled to sit up, and as he did, he saw Katherine standing near him. Then North appeared next to her. They beckoned him to join them.

They spoke, but he could not hear them. He

could only hear the mysterious voice from long ago: "I believe. I believe. I believe."

Then suddenly, he woke up. He looked around his library, startled. He could still hear the voice, but only the owls were there.

And for the second time he felt the minds of Katherine and North reaching out to him. Their thoughts and his had become connected. He felt— no, he knew—that they were in grave danger and that he must act instantly.

He grabbed the box that held Nightlight's moonbeam and the broken bits of the diamond dagger. Then he waved his staff over the new stacks of books. He felt strong again. Young again. Like Ombric in days of yore. Could he project himself to the Earth's core? In an instant! And the books? Absolutely! His friends needed him! The peace he felt in his dream could come later.

But that voice from the past . . . the voice that had saved him on that fateful day when he first learned the glory and terror of magic. It sounded so familiar now.

Who—or *what*—was it?

CHAPTER THIRTY

In Which All Is Linked by an Ancient Mind Trick That Has a Most Surprising Origin

NORTH WAS DAZZLED. BUNNYMUND was a madman, or rabbit, or whatever . . . a dervish! A devil! A juggernaut! There simply wasn't a way to describe the Pooka's electrifying deeds. He had taken his relic and fixed it to the end of his staff, then aimed it at the lead wall that blocked their way. If this ancient lead had never seen sunlight, starlight, or any light other than lava light before, it was seeing it now. The light that the relic contained blistered forth from a thousand tiny holes that opened up from its shell. This light would *not* be blocked or consumed; it could peel back the dense lead as smoothly as sealing wax from parchment.

But still, North felt wary—it was almost *too* easy. The Fearlings kept retreating without putting up much of a fight. They were going deeper and deeper into the Earth's core, and the wavy, peculiar lead-and-lava landscape was hard to mark or remember. North prided himself on his stellar sense of direction, but he now felt uncertain about how to find his way back out, and his warrior's instincts were telling him he was being pulled into an ambush.

It was at just that moment that there came a sort of ringing in his ears, the sensation blocking out the clatter of battle around him. He looked to Bunny-mund, and he knew that the Pooka was experiencing the same sensation.

The magic sword could feel it too. The mirror

emerged again from its hilt, and North could see Katherine's face in it. Her lips did not move, but he could hear her voice. "There is no time to tell you everything. We must call Ombric here now!" she said. "He needs us, and we need him. Pitch has made a trap for you."

But how can we call Ombric? North wondered. Then he remembered when they were back in Santoff Claussen, when he had felt their minds unite as one. He knew that he must concentrate to make their minds combine again. Despite the skirmish going on around him, he closed his eyes, and all became quiet except for his and Katherine's voices: *I believe . . . I believe . . . I believe.* Then he heard Bunnymund's voice join theirs! And this surprised North. They had a new ally, a new friend.

But then North saw Ombric in the sword's

mirror. He was lying in a field of grass. He looked sad, old, as if he were dying. It scared North, and he could tell it did the same to Katherine and Bunnymund. So they shouted out to him, their minds as one, "Believe, believe, believe. You are needed!"

The mirror went bright, then Ombric was no longer visible. North heard Katherine say, "Be cautious. Wait for Ombric. Wait for me." Then the mirror went dark again.

North turned to Bunnymund, who was smiling.

"I haven't done the Pookan mind meld in centuries. I didn't know you and the girl knew how."

"Neither did we," North confessed.

"Even better," replied the Pooka. And off he hopped, like some warrior-rabbit-buffalo.

North had no choice but to follow.

CHAPTER THIRTY-ONE

The Mad Scramble

NORTH, BUNNYMUND, AND THE Warrior Eggs continued their push into the depths of Pitch's lair. Now mindful of the trap they were entering, Bunnymund left small groups of men (or, rather, eggs) to help mark their way out and to sound the alarm if an ambush was coming.

But the Fearlings continued to pull back, now without fighting at all.

"Something is definitely up, Bunnymund," said North.

"I'd say Pitch is making a tactical change

in his plans," the Pooka agreed.

"Do we split our forces?" wondered North.

"One of us goes forward to investigate while the other watches his back?" suggested Bunnymund.

"You read my mind," North said jokingly.

"Yes," replied the Pooka, "but only when I think it necessary."

North wasn't sure if Bunnymund was kidding or not, but before he could ask, the hulking rabbit gave him a good-natured shove. "Now, get going, my friend; you wanted Pitch to yourself."

North shot the rabbit a glance as he led half the eggs toward the heart of Pitch's hideout. "Come hopping if you hear anything," he called over his shoulder.

The Pooka decided to let North have the last word. He didn't mind the human's rabbit jokes at his expense. It had been at least seven hundred years since anybody had made any sort of jest to him. He'd almost forgotten the peculiar pleasures of kidding and being kidded, and how humans used humor to help them not be afraid.

And there was much to fear in this place.

With spears, swords, and clubs at the ready, North led a tight formation of eggs cautiously forward. The Fearling troops were continuing to back away, their clattering armor sending waves of uneasy echoes through the tunnel. It was dim—only the blue glint of the lead lava flows provided any light.

Then North heard the Nightmare King bellow, "Come forward!"

North's sword automatically tightened around his hand, but its glow stayed pale—North could tell it was doing all it could to avoid making him an easy target in this twilight.

Then they came to a huge open chamber. Great swirling lead columns formed a sort of circular shape to the room. The columns widened at the top as they merged into what could be called the ceiling.

Behind the lead columns, North could see only heavily armored Fearlings, a vast army of gray menace that completely surrounded the chamber and seemed eager to attack.

In the room's center, Pitch was standing triumphantly among every book from Ombric's library. They were stacked haphazardly in tall piles on the uneven floor of the chamber. North could see *The History of Levitation While Eating, Mysteries of Vanishing Keys*, and Ombric's beloved books on Atlantis. *What is the old man up to?* North wondered. Pitch gazed greedily from book to book, then grabbed one and began to scan its contents. He smiled to himself, then looked up at North, staring at him with gleeful hate.

North matched Pitch's stare, while, from the corner of his eye, he saw the children of Santoff Claussen huddled in cages that hung from lead beams.

Ombric was nowhere in sight, so North knew to bide his time and wait till the wizard made his play. North realized Pitch was expecting him to say something—explain the arrival of the books or demand that the children be released.

But North kept steady and quiet, as only the smartest warriors did. Let *the villain* make the first move.

"Why send a thief to do a Pooka's job?" Pitch asked mockingly.

North said not a word; he just moved in closer, the eggs at his side. He raised his sword as if to strike.

"Where'd you steal *that?*" Pitch questioned, suddenly curious. "It's a sword for a king, not a Cossack criminal."

North stayed silent. The magic sword glowed. Pitch, however, did not reach for his own weapon, but instead held out one of Ombric's books.

"At ease, brigand. I've got what I asked for. The books are here." Pitch turned to a Fearling. "Release the children," he ordered.

The Fearling unlocked the swaying cages, and the children jumped out. They tried to run to North, but the Fearling unsheathed his sword and brought it down in front of them, blocking their way.

Pointing to the sealed solid lead cage, Tall William shouted, "Katherine and Nightlight are in there!"

North inched closer, but still he said nothing. His sword glowed even brighter.

"No need to attack, Cossack," Pitch said soothingly. "The books are here. A deal is a deal. We can part and fight another day. Yes?"

North eyed him suspiciously. *Could this work without a fight?*

"But . . . ," Pitch continued, "I must be sure these books are what they seem." And he began to read a spell.

North knew that the incantation was directed at him. What would Pitch do? Turn him into a fungus, a slave, a Fearling general? He prepared to charge, but the sword held him back! He pushed against it, but it would not budge.

Then he remembered what Yaloo the Yeti had told him: "Perhaps the weapon is fighting *for* you."

The sword must know something, North decided.

Pitch, on the other hand, was growing angry.

Something was evidently not going as he wished.

Pitch repeated the spell from the book slowly, carefully, as if testing each syllable. Then North understood: The spell was useless; the books were sabotaged!

Pitch tried another spell. Then another. He snatched up the book of enslavement spells and read the words he knew by heart. "They're all fake!" he bellowed. "FAKE!"

North readied to strike. From behind him, he

could hear the charge of Bunnymund and his troops. Pitch threw the book down and unsheathed his sword.

The room exploded into chaos.

The Fearlings rushed North. The earsplitting clash of two armies bent on destroying each other filled the chamber. Then the Pookan war cry sounded out above the din—Bunnymund had arrived, his relic staff sending beams of light crisscrossing the room, engulfing the Fearlings.

The room was furious with spears, swords, clubs, arrows, and armor. North was amazed. The Warrior Eggs were incredibly agile fighters. They could roll, leap, and charge with lightning speed, and their armor was most difficult to penetrate. Their weapons were injected with the ancient light of the egg relic and more than held their own against the Fearlings.

North kept own his sights on Pitch, who was moving toward the children. North's sword glowed red; it was time to strike. He charged through the dense clusters of Fearlings and Warrior Eggs, easily felling every enemy that blocked his way.

Pitch was opening his cape. It rippled out and began to surround the children. North ran up the huge stack of books in front of him like it was a staircase, then leaped from the top, his sword at the ready, sailing over Pitch. Pitch's cape was curling around the children like a pair of massive claws, but before he could close it, North landed between them: Villain and thief were face-to-face, swords drawn.

North said to his sword, "Do what needs doing." With two deft swings, he sliced away the cape on either side of Pitch. The children were free! But in that one moment of victory, North's guard was down, and Pitch did his worst.

North staggered backward, gasping. The handle of Pitch's saber protruded from his side; the tip jutted out from the back of his coat. He'd been run through.

The children screamed. Pitch grinned. He pulled his sword back out. But North would not go down yet. He gripped his magic sword and it responded. It glowed with such brightness.

It was then that miracles occurred.

Nightlight's cage exploded open and light poured from it. The entire chamber was awash with light. The armor-covered Fearlings were almost blinded. Pitch pulled the cowl of his hood forward to block his face from the glare.

North charged again. Despite his wounds, despite the wrenching pain, he could feel an amazing power surge from the magic sword into him. It was almost as if the sword could remember Pitch and was eager to finish him. With indescribable fury, North hacked and lunged at the Nightmare King.

But Pitch had grown stronger since last they'd met, and even with the power of the magic sword, North was unable to best him. His wound was hampering him; he felt himself weakening. Then he saw the djinni, discarded in the corner. Without Pitch inside it, perhaps it would still heed his command.

"Djinni!" North shouted. "Attack him!" The djinni immediately stiffened and then ran toward North. It picked up two swords that were dropped in the battle. Was it coming to help or hinder?

The djinni attacked Pitch! *Now we've a chance,* North thought with relief.

When he next looked up, he was stunned to see

Ombric there as well, swinging at Pitch with his staff and landing more blows than North would have ever expected from the old wizard. Then Bunnymund literally came flying into the room, his ears twirling with such speed that they held him aloft like a helicopter. With the relic at the end of his lance, he charged Pitch like a jousting knight.

But Pitch was their match. He shouted out to the Fearlings and they began to merge into him. He grew bigger and stronger, their armor adding layer after layer atop his. Now Pitch was truly a monster in size as well as spirit.

The children huddled into a corner. They could see what was happening—even without Ombric's books of spells, Pitch seemed unbeatable. Fear crept into their hearts.

Then from the lead cage there shot another bolt

of light, and a shimmering, perfect laugh pierced the noise of the battle like an arrow.

Nightlight's laugh!

Nightlight flew straight toward Pitch, with Katherine riding on his back. His staff was outstretched, the diamond dagger repaired and aimed at Pitch's heart.

North caught a glimpse of them as they streaked toward Pitch. *Outstanding*, he thought. *The boy will do him in.*

But Nightlight pulled up short, hovering just within reach of Pitch's sword.

What is he doing?! North thought, pausing in mid-swing. "His heart, boy!" he shouted. "Strike him in the heart!"

Still Nightlight held back. Pitch, however, did not. He sliced savagely at Nightlight, but the spectral boy parried his blow, and his diamond dagger shattered

Pitch's sword. Now North and the others could move in for the kill.

But before they could strike, Katherine raised up her hand and held something out toward Pitch. Not a weapon—no, it was something she wanted him to see. *What is she holding?* North strained to look. The locket! With the picture of Pitch's daughter!

For a moment time seemed to stand still.

Pitch stared at the locket, his face twisted and monstrous. His gaze did not waver from the picture. Then his face began to change, the anger and fury fading, replaced by a look that was mournful, anguished, and unbearably sad. North and the others held steady, hardly believing what they were seeing. The King of the Nightmares was no longer horrifying but horrified. He reached out with his damaged hand—the one he had used to try to change

Nightlight into a Fearling, the hand that now looked human. He tugged the locket away from Katherine, and for an instant she felt his hand against hers. His touch was not of a creature of fear. It was the touch of a father who had lost his child. Pitch let out a long and haunted scream that came from the depths of whatever sort of a soul he still had.

He looked at the picture for one more moment, then faded, vanishing completely away. The Fearling Army disappeared with him.

And the battle was over.

CHAPTER THIRTY-TWO

North Is Fallen

THERE WAS A SUDDEN and strange calm in the chamber. There they were, together at last, the heroes of the battle at the Earth's core. Such an amazing and unlikely group: a spectral boy, a girl, a Cossack, an ancient wizard, a metal djinni, a huge Rabbit Man, and an army of Warrior Eggs. The children ran to the comfort of their friends and protectors. But North winced as the littlest William rushed into his arms. He grabbed at his wound, then dropped his sword and fell to one knee.

Ombric and Katherine hurried to his side. "How

bad is it, lad?" asked Ombric, bending close. North could not answer. As they laid him down, his face grew paler and even more drained of color. His sword lay next to him. It seemed to dim and darken. Katherine took his hand. It felt cold. North looked up at her as she began to cry.

CHAPTER THIRTY-THREE

The Bookworm Turns

It WAS A BEAUTIFUL afternoon in the enchanted woods that surrounded Santoff Claussen. The children of the village were playing their favorite new game, called "Battle at the Earth's Core." The massive trees that edged the small open grove had bent their branches down in ways that looked like the lead columns of Pitch's lair. William the Almost Youngest was pretending to be Ombric, Tall William was Bunnymund, Fog was the djinni, and Petter was Nightlight. The bear was Pitch, which worked very well, as he was so large and very good at tussling with the children with just enough wildness that it was really fun. Plus, he was very difficult to hurt by accident.

A group of squirrels pretended to be the children, dressed up in tiny clothes that matched what they had been wearing during the battle. The birds of the forest were the Fearlings, and a number of actual Warrior Eggs (a gift from Bunnymund) played themselves.

William the Absolute Youngest always wanted to be North; he loved North so much, and it was he who had last hugged North before he fell.

Petter yelled for Katherine to join them, to play her own character, but she did not answer. She rarely joined in this game—she'd lived it, after all, so she didn't need to play it. Petter's sister Sascha gladly took her place.

Katherine was up in the topmost branches of Big

Root. She had made a small, ramshackle tree house in the crook at the highest point. She went to it often now. She could be alone there to think and to remember.

She spent her time making stories out of what she had seen. Sometimes she even wrote short little rhymes of their adventures. There was an egg that had fallen from a wall of Pitch's chamber during the battle. She was sure he would break, but his armor had protected him. If only the same could have been said for North. He had fallen. And no one had thought he could be made whole again.

Today she was combining those two stories into a rhyme, drawing pictures of a great egg that had shattered and couldn't be put back together again. She would sometimes make stories that were different from what had happened but were about how she felt or what she wished had been. This was a new way of thinking for her, and she loved it—needed to do it. These stories had become a mysterious new force in her, a way of healing and understanding the wonders and sorrows of her wild new life.

She was never actually alone in the tree house. Kailash would fly her up there and nap quietly as Katherine wrote, her long neck wrapped around the girl as she leaned against the soft, feathered body.

And there was one more companion with her: Mr. Qwerty. Or at least what he had become.

When Nightlight had told Mr. Qwerty to eat the library to save it from Pitch—yes, it had been Nightlight's idea—something remarkable had happened. The spells and magic contained in the thousands of pages had transformed the glowworm. In his cocoon he had changed, but it was not into a butterfly. He became instead something that the world had never seen before. He had wings, many of them, but they were made of paper—he had become a sort of living book! His pages were all blank. It was on these pages that Katherine wrote her stories.

Katherine could hear her friends playing in the woods. They were making a story too, of that great and terrible battle. It always changed as they acted it out. Sometimes whoever played Bunnymund would come too later, or the bear would run off too soon, or the squirrels would decide that they wanted to join in the battle and escape from the "cages" too early. But one part always stayed the same: when North fell. Somehow, it seemed important to do that part exactly as it had happened.

As Katherine sat in her tree house, she heard

her friends readying for their game's final battle. She stopped her writing to listen.

Down in the forest William the Absolute Youngest had fallen to the ground, the stick that was his pretend sword lying at his side. Sascha, Fog, Petter, and the others stood over him as he seemed to die. Then he reached for his magic sword.

Suddenly, a voice came booming from the trees at the edge of the clearing.

"No! No! No!" yelled Nicholas St. North. He came striding toward them. "That's not how it happened! Bunnymund gave me that magic chocolate first."

North came up to them looking very hale and hearty. He carried with him a large sack thrown over his shoulder.

"The magic chocolate saved me, I grabbed the

sword, and it began to glow again," he reminded them.

"But our stick sword can't glow for real," explained the youngest William.

"Well, this one can," replied North cheerfully as he dumped the sack upside down. Toy swords and staffs and relics and costumes spilled out on the ground before them. "I made them this morning. Well, the djinni helped a bit."

The children were delighted with their gifts. They grabbed their different costumes and weaponry and prepared to continue their game.

Katherine flew down on Kailash. She wanted to watch how her friends would act out the rest of the events now that they had props.

Bunnymund came popping out of the ground nearby, Ombric with him. The two had become close collaborators since the battle, once Ombric had discovered that it was Bunnymund who had saved him that long-ago day when he had tried his first magic. They traded spells and histories of this and that. He felt a strong kinship with the Rabbit Man—the only creature alive who was older and wiser than himself. Being with this marvelous creature made Ombric feel younger, almost like a student again.

The two of them stopped a moment and watched the children's game unfold. "So how exactly does the chocolate transform you, Bunnymund?" Ombric asked his new friend.

"My dear fellow," the rabbit replied, "I'm not entirely sure. Some mysteries need no solution. Does it help to understand why rainbows happen?"

"I think it does," replied Ombric.

The rabbit almost laughed. "You humans."

And from the trees above, a brave and gentle

spirit watched them all. Nightlight, the one who said the least but perhaps knew the most, thought only of the comfort he felt. He was among true friends. The moonbeam, back inside the diamond dagger, was happy as well. The dagger was bigger now. It contained the tears that Nightlight had taken from the children when they'd been kidnapped; he'd used them to bind the broken dagger back together again. Nightlight had always known that taking the sorrows of those you love makes you stronger in the end.

Remembering this now made him glow a bit brighter. Katherine could sense his gaze. She turned and looked up. She could not see him—he was hiding—but she knew he was there. The power of friendship was magical indeed. The happiness Nightlight felt spread to all of them. They had done what good friends should do: They had all saved one another. Whatever trials or troubles might come, from now on, their bond would be unbreakable. They were of one mind and heart.

And that heart would beat forever. Past time and tide and stories yet told.

Acknowledgments

Huzzahs all around to
Elizabeth Blake-Linn, Caitlyn Dlouhy,
Trish Farnsworth-Smith, Jeannie Ng, and Lauren Rille,
and with special appreciation to Laurie Calkhoven—
Guardians of the Book, all.

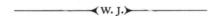

—————————⟨W. J.⟩—— ————

TURN THE PAGE FOR A SNEAK PEEK

AT THE NEXT CHAPTER IN OUR ONGOING SAGA,

TOOTHIANA

QUEEN OF THE TOOTH FAIRY ARMIES

—◆—

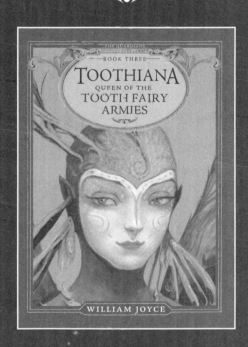

THE GUARDIANS

BOOK THREE

TOOTHIANA
QUEEN OF THE
TOOTH FAIRY
ARMIES

WILLIAM JOYCE

The Changes That Come with Peace

WILLIAM THE ABSOLUTE YOUNGEST galloped through the enchanted village of Santoff Claussen on the back of a large Warrior Egg, a gift from E. Aster Bunnymund. "I can't stop or I'll be scrambled!" he shouted over his shoulder to his friend Fog. In this new game of Warrior Egg tag, to be scrambled meant you had been caught by the opposing egg team and therefore, had lost a point.

Sascha and her brother, Petter, were in hot pursuit, riding Warrior Eggs of their own. The matchstick-thin legs of the mechanical eggs moved so fast, they were a blur.

"Comin' in for the scramble shot!" Petter warned. His long tag pole, with the egg-shaped tip, was inches away from Sascha.

"Eat my yolk," Sascha said with a triumphant laugh. She pushed a button, and suddenly, her Warrior Egg sprouted wings. She flew over the others, reaching the finish line first.

William the Absolute Youngest slowed to a trot. "Wings!" he grumbled. "They aren't even in the rules!"

"I invented them yesterday," said Sascha. "There's nothing in the rules that says you can't use 'em."

Soon Sascha was helping the youngest William construct his own set of eggbot wings. She liked the youngest William. He always tried to act older, and she appreciated his determination and spirit. Petter and Fog, feeling wild and industrious, catapulted themselves to the hollow of a tall tree where they had

erected a hideout devoted to solving ancient mysteries, such as: why was there such a thing as bedtime,
and what could they do to eliminate it forever?

Across the clearing, in a tree house perched high
in the branches of Big Root—the tree at the center of
the village—their friend Katherine contently watched
the children play.

The air shimmered with their happy laughter.
Many months had passed since the battle at the
Earth's core during which Pitch, the Nightmare King,
had been soundly defeated by Katherine and the
other Guardians: Ombric, the wizard; his apprentice,
Nicholas St. North; their friend Nightlight; and their
newest ally, the Pookan rabbit known as E. Aster
Bunnymund. Pitch, who had hungered for the dreams
of innocent children and longed to replace them with
nightmares, had vowed with his Fearlings to make

all the children of Earth live in terror. But since the great battle, he had not been seen or heard from, and Katherine was beginning to hope that Pitch had been vanquished forever.

As for Katherine and her battle mates, their lives were forever changed. The Man in the Moon himself had given them the title of "Guardians." They were heroes now, sworn to protect the children of not just Santoff Claussen, but the entire planet. They had defeated Pitch, and their greatest challenge at present was how to manage the peace. The "nightmare" of Pitch's reign seemed to be over.

The other children of the village now filled their days with mischief and magic. Bunnymund, who could burrow through the Earth with astonishing speed, had created a series of tunnels for them, connecting the village with his home on Easter Island and with other amazing outposts around the world, and the children had become intrepid explorers. On any given day they might journey to the African savanna to visit the lions, cheetahs, and hippopotami—Ombric had taught them a number of animal languages, so they had numerous stories to hear and tell. Many of the creatures had already heard of their amazing adventures.

The children also regularly circled through Easter Island for the latest chocolate confection Bunnymund had invented, and could still be back in time for dinner and games with Bunnymund's mechanical egg comrades. The eggs were once Bunnymund's warriors; now they helped the children build all manner of interesting contraptions, from intricate egg-shaped puzzles where every piece was egg-shaped (a nearly impossible and frankly unexplainable feat) to egg-shaped submarines. But no matter where the children roamed or what they did to occupy their days, whenever they returned home to Santoff Claussen, it had never seemed so lovely to them.

As Katherine sat in her tree house, she put her arm around Kailash, her great Himalayan Snow Goose, and looked out on her beloved village. The forest that surrounded and protected Santoff Claussen had bloomed into a kind of eternal spring. The massive oaks and vines that had once formed an impenetrable wall against the outside world were thick with leaves of the deepest green. The huge, spear-size thorns that had once covered the vines grew pliant and blossomed with sweet-scented flowers.

Katherine loved the smell, and drew a deep breath of it. In the distance she could see Nicholas St. North walking with the beautiful, ephemeral Spirit of the Forest. She was more radiant now than ever before. Her gossamer robes were resplendent with blooms that shimmered like jewels. North was deep in conversation with her, so Katherine decided to investigate. She climbed on to Kailash's back and flew down into the clearing, just in time to see William the

Absolute Youngest try out the new wings with which he'd outfitted his Warrior Egg. He landed and trotted over to her.

"Want to race with us, Katherine?" he asked. He gave Kailash a scratch on her neck, and the goose honked a hello.

"I will later!" Katherine said, smiling. She waved to her friends and headed into the forest, realizing that it had been quite some time since any of the children had asked her to play, and an even longer time since she had accepted. In joining the world of the Guardians, she was in a strange new phase of her life—where she was neither child nor adult. As she watched the youngest William fly away with Sascha close behind him, she couldn't help but feel a bit torn.

Then she heard North's hearty laugh and, underneath that, the more musical tones of the Spirit of the Forest. Katherine hurried toward them, thinking that it was hard to believe that when North first came to Santoff Claussen with his band of outlaws, it had been with the intent to steal its treasures. The Spirit of the Forest, the village's last line of defense, had turned North's crew of cutthroats and bandits into stone statues—hideous, hunched elves. But she had spared North, for he alone among them was pure of heart.

When Katherine caught up with the Spirit and North, they were standing in that most strange and eerie part of the forest—the place where North's men stood frozen in time, like stones in a forgotten burial site. With the Spirit's help, North was bringing his bandits back to human form.

As the Spirit touched the head of each statue, North repeated the same spell, "From flesh to stone and back again. To serve with honor, your one true friend." And one by one they emerged from their frozen poses. To North's great amusement, they hadn't regained their size. They were still the same height as their stone selves—about two feet tall, with bulbous noses and high, childlike voices.

"Welcome back," North called out, slapping each of the elfin men on the back.

The men stamped their little feet and waved their little arms to get their blood flowing again, and soon the children, drawn by North's laughter, arrived. They were shocked; they often played among these small stone men, and now that they were moving—were alive, in fact—the children were most intrigued. Tall William, the first son of Old William, towered over them. Even the youngest William was overjoyed—at last he was taller than someone else.

While the children watched, the little men kneeled before North. They took on new names as they pledged to follow their former outlaw leader in a new life of goodness. Gregor of the Mighty Stink became Gregor of the Mighty Smile. Sergei the Terrible was now Sergei the Giggler, and so on.

It was an odd but auspicious moment, especially for North. He remembered his wild, unruly life as a bandit and the many dark deeds that he and these fellows had committed. He'd become a hero, a man of great learning, good humor, and some wisdom. So much had changed since that moment when he faced the temptation of the Spirit of the Forest, when he had rejected her promises of treasure and had chosen to save the children of Santoff Claussen.

North turned and looked at young Katherine. He felt the full weight of all they had been through. They had both changed. It was a change he did not fully understand, but he knew he was glad for it. For though these dwarfish fellows in front of him had once been his comrades in crime, North, in his heart, had been alone. But that was past. This was a different day. And through the friendship he now knew, he could change bad men to good and stone back to flesh.

North gently asked his old confederates to rise. They did so gladly.

Peace had indeed come.

Katherine took North's hand, and together they welcomed these baffled little men to the world of Santoff Claussen.

The Guardians Gather

ALTHOUGH THE CHILDREN HAD begun to refer to the battle at the Earth's core as "Pitch's Last Battle," the Guardians knew that the Nightmare King was both devious and shrewd. He could still be lurking somewhere, ready to pounce.

Nightlight, the mysterious, otherworldly boy who was Katherine's dearest friend, scoured the night sky for signs of Pitch's army. He even traveled deep into the cave where he'd been imprisoned in Pitch's icy heart for centuries, but all he found were memories of those dark times. Of Pitch and his Fearling soldiers, he could find not even an echo. Bunnymund kept his rabbit ears tuned for ominous signs while burrowing his system of tunnels, and Ombric cast his mind about for bits of dark magic that might be creeping into the world. As for North, he was being rather secretive. He kept to himself (or, rather, to his elfin friends), working quietly and diligently in the great study, deep at the center of Big Root. On what he was working, no one knew for sure, but he seemed most intense.

And every night the children clamored for Mr. Qwerty, the glowworm who had transformed himself

into a magical book. Because he had eaten every book in Ombric's library, he could tell the children any fact or story they wanted to hear. Mr.

Qwerty's pages were blank, at least until he began to read himself, and then the words and drawings would appear. But most nights the children wanted to hear one of Katherine's stories from Mr. Qwerty, for he allowed only her to write in him. But before any story was read, Katherine asked them about their dreams. Not one had had a single nightmare since the great battle.

There truly was *absolutely* no sign of Pitch. The sun seemed to shine brighter, every day seemed more beautiful, perfect, carefree. It was as if, when Pitch vanished, he took all the evil in the world with him.

Even so, the Guardians knew that wickedness of Pitch's magnitude did not surrender easily. They met together every day, never at an appointed time, but when it somehow seemed right. Their bond of friendship was so strong that it now connected them in heart and mind. Each could often sense what the others felt, and when it felt like the time to gather, they would just somehow *know*. They would drop what they were doing and go to Big Root, where, with cups of tea, they'd discuss any possible signs of Pitch's return.

On this particular day Nightlight hadn't far to travel. The night before, he'd stayed in Big Root's tree-top all through the night, having searched every corner of the globe at dusk and found nothing alarming. Though he could fly forever, and never slept, his habit was to watch over Katherine and Kailash. More and more often the girl and her goose slept in their nest-like tree house, and so Nightlight would join them and guard them till morning.

Among the Guardians, his and Katherine's bond was the greatest. It hovered in a lovely realm that went past words and descriptions. The two never tired of the other's company and felt a pang of sadness when apart. But even that ache was somehow exquisite, for they knew that they would never be separated for long. Nightlight would never let that be so. Nor would Katherine. Time and time again they had managed a way to find each other, no matter how desperate the circumstances.

So Nightlight felt most perfectly at peace when watching over Katherine as she slept. Sleep was a mystery to him, and in some ways, so was dreaming. It worried him, in fact. Katherine was there but not entirely. Her mind traveled to Dreamlands where he could not follow.

In his childish way, he longed to go with her. And on this night, he had found a way to trespass into the unknown realm of her sleeping mind.

As he'd sat beside Katherine and her goose as they slept, he'd looked up to the Moon. His friend was full and bright. In these peaceful times the playful moonbeams came to him less often than before. There were no worries or urgent messages from the Man in the Moon, and so Nightlight could now enjoy the silent beauty of his benefactor. But a glint of something on Katherine's cheek had reflected the Moon's glow. Nightlight leaned in closely.

It was a tear. A tear? This confounded him. What was there in her dream that would make Katherine cry? He knew about the power of tears. It was from tears that his diamond dagger was forged. But those tears were from wakeful times. He had never touched a Dream Tear. But before he could think better of it, he reached down and gently plucked it up.

Dream Tears are very powerful, and when

Nightlight first tried to look into it, he was nearly knocked from the tree. He caught his balance and carefully looked at the small drop. Inside was Katherine's dream. And what he saw there seared his soul. For the first time in all his strange and dazzling life, Nightlight felt a deep, unsettling fear.

There, haunting her dreams, he had seen Pitch.

Nightlight and the Dream Tear

Nightlight Must Lie

Now, as Nightlight shimmered his way into the waiting room of Big Root, he was the last to arrive. He kept his distance, perching high on one of the bookcases. Ombric and Bunnymund were poring over a map of the lost city of Atlantis. Katherine spied Nightlight and could tell immediately that something was troubling him.

North began regaling Ombric with the news about his band of brigands and their new lives as elfin helpers.

Ombric's left eyebrow rose high; he was clearly

amused. "Well done, Nicholas. I see great things in store for your little men," he said.

Though neither man would say out loud how they felt, Katherine could tell Ombric was immensely proud of his apprentice, and North took great pleasure in Ombric's approval. She felt a surge of happiness for the both of them.

Bunnymund's ears twitched. *These humans and their emotions,* he thought. *They are so odd. They are more interested in feelings than chocolate!*

"Any sign of Pitch today?" he asked politely but pointedly.

North shook his head. "The old grump hasn't grumbled."

"None of the children have had bad dreams," reported Katherine.

Nightlight didn't respond. He knew otherwise.

Or, at least, he thought he did.

Bunnymund then answered his own question. "And nothing in my tunnels—nothing evil or unchocolatey or anti-egg anywhere."

Ombric stroked his beard. "Perhaps the children are correct," he mused, "and the battle at the Earth's core truly was Pitch's *last* battle."

North pondered. "Can that really be?"

Katherine turned to Nightlight. She generally knew what he was thinking, but today she couldn't read him. "Nightlight," she prompted, "have you seen anything?"

He shifted on his perch. His brow furrowed, but he shook his head.

It was the first time Nightlight had ever lied.